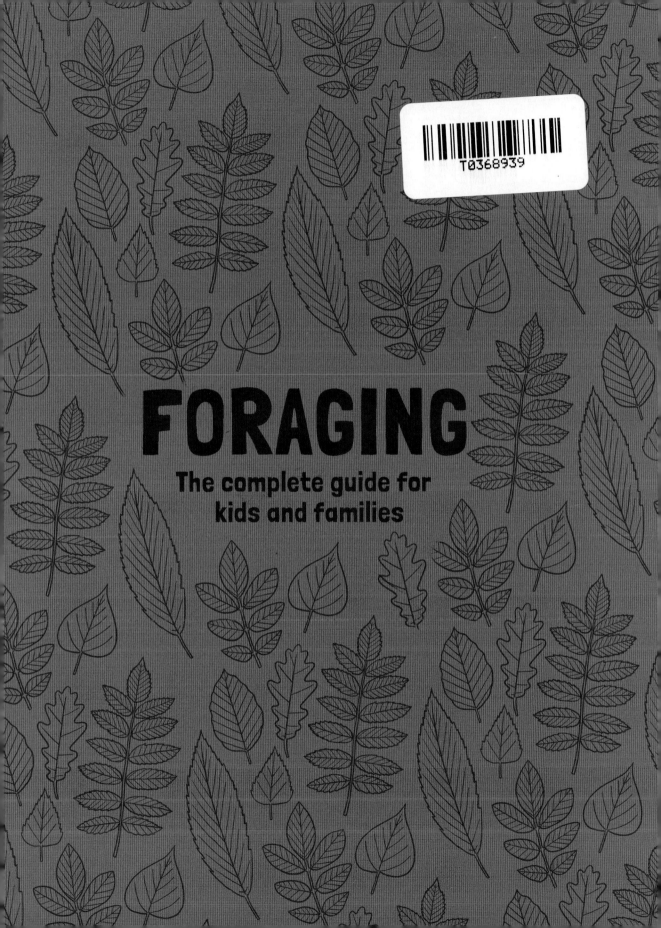

FORAGING

The complete guide for kids and families

T0368939

ABOUT THE AUTHORS

As children, Dane and Stella De Luca Mulandiee were inspired by the natural world. They have now spent many years creating educational content together on everything they love and believe in, from foraging to folklore. Their bestselling book *Knowledge To Forage* shot to fame in the summer of 2022, launching their careers as authors. They live in Peacehaven with their four children and two dogs.

Stella and Dane De Luca Mulandiee

FORAGING

The complete guide for kids and families

Illustrated by Elly Jahnz

PUFFIN

PUFFIN BOOKS

UK | USA | Canada | Ireland | Australia
India | New Zealand | South Africa

Puffin Books is part of the Penguin Random House group of companies
whose addresses can be found at global.penguinrandomhouse.com

www.penguin.co.uk
www.puffin.co.uk
www.ladybird.co.uk

 Penguin
Random House
UK

First published 2024
Adapted from *Knowledge to Forage* © Stella and Dane De Luca Mulandiee, 2022

001

Text copyright © Stella and Dane De Luca Mulandiee, 2024
Illustrations copyright © Elly Jahnz, 2024
Stock illustrations © Adobe Stock Image Library
All photographic images © Stella and Dane De Luca Mulandiee
With thanks to Lucy Doncaster for editorial and writing contributions

The moral right of the authors and illustrator has been asserted

Page design by Sophie Stericker
Printed and bound in Malaysia

The authorized representative in the EEA is Penguin Random House Ireland, Morrison Chambers,
32 Nassau Street, Dublin D02 YH68

A CIP catalogue record for this book is available from the British Library

ISBN: 978–0–241–65456–9

All correspondence to:
Puffin Books
Penguin Random House Children's
One Embassy Gardens, 8 Viaduct Gardens, London SW11 7BW

FSC
www.fsc.org
MIX
Paper | Supporting
responsible forestry
FSC® C018179

Dedicated to our four lovely children.
For trudging through the countryside in rain and shine,
and teaching us as much about life as we've taught them.
D & S DLM

To Sebbie, always keep exploring.
And to Aaron, for your support and patience.
EJ

Contents

We've divided the various plants, trees, fruits and flowers in this book into different sections to make it easier to find what you're looking for. But nature isn't divided up into neat sections! For example, some fruits grow on bushes and some grow on trees. We hope that our way of organizing the book will still be a useful tool when navigating the great outdoors.

Plants and Bushes 58

Flowers 100

Trees 154

A Note to our Readers

The information in this book is intended as a general guide and believed to be correct as at April 2022, but is not to be relied on in law and is subject to change. The activities described in this book are undertaken at the participants' own risk. For safe outdoor activity, children should be accompanied by an appropriate adult and particular care should be taken to avoid poisonous plants. Children should be supervised in the kitchen at all times and appropriate kitchen safety measures used. The recipes in this book may not be suitable for those with certain food allergies or intolerances. Please check the recipes carefully for the presence of any ingredients or substances which may cause an adverse reaction if consumed by those with a food allergy or intolerance. The author and publishers disclaim, as far as the law allows, any liability arising directly or indirectly from the use or misuse of any information contained in this book.

The information and reference guides in this book are intended solely for the general information of the reader. The contents of this book are not intended to offer personal medical advice, diagnose health problems, or for treatment purposes. This book is not a substitute for medical care provided by a licensed and qualified health professional. Please consult your health care provider for any advice on medications and medical issues.

Extra Care Needed

 When you see this symbol, you need to take extra care! Ensure you read everything really carefully, and have your adult on hand to help.

WELCOME TO THE WORLD OF FORAGING

When you think of foraging, you probably think about looking for wild food. This is certainly what foraging is, and what a lot of this book is about! But foraging is a lot more than that. It's a reason to be out in the woods; it leads us off the beaten track and helps us to experience the natural world in a way we may not have done before. Foraging teaches us to look, hear, feel and taste, and opens our eyes to the wonders that grow wild and free all around us.

This is a book full of memories, fun, education and fresh air. It's about coming together with friends, family and the loved ones in your life, and enjoying everything nature has to offer. It will help you to disconnect from technology – phones, the internet, the TV – and connect with each other.

So what are you waiting for?
Put on your boots, grab a bag and get
ready to dive into the world of foraging!

Dane

Maddox

Maddie

Bruce

Kenny

Meet the family!

We're a close family, with the firm belief that all the best things in life are wild and free. So much so, in fact, that we've spent many years creating guides to foraging and getting outdoors.

Why? Because we felt guides like this didn't exist – at least not in a way we could confidently and easily understand. So, we took everything we'd learnt about foraging and put it on YouTube, which meant anyone who wanted to find out more could have access to it for free.

Now, as well as educational videos, we create books that teach foraging (our first big book of foraging was called *Knowledge to Forage*), herbalism, natural history, crafts and how to make fun and easy recipes. You can find all our free educational videos on our YouTube channel, Home Is Where Our Heart Is, which contains many video guides on the plants, trees and recipes featured in this book. It's a great way to get to know us, so be sure to check it out!

YouTube: @ homeiswhereourheartis
Instagram: @home_is_where_our_heart_is
Website: www.home-is-where-our-heart-is.co.uk

OUR FAMILY ARE HERE TO TEACH YOU ALL ABOUT FORAGING. YOU'LL SEE US POP UP NOW AND AGAIN!

Duke

Bjorn

Stella

HOW TO USE THIS BOOK

We want foraging to be as fun and easy as possible, so we've divided this book into sections to help you. We start off with a few basics about what foraging is, why it's so great, and how to do it safely (plus some hints and tips for cooking, and a bit of help with plant names). There's then a guide packed with information about where to find some of the most commonly foraged foods in the UK – from fruits, plants and bushes to flowers and trees.

As well as fun facts and top tips, these pages include stories about the plants and trees, and information about herbalism, an ancient form of medicine (sometimes called 'traditional medicine' or 'herbal medicine') that uses parts of a plant (often known as 'medicinal herbs') in a way that was once thought to cure body and mind. To help you stay safe, there's also a chapter on poisonous plants to watch out for.

At the back of the book, we take a deep dive into the benefits of forest bathing and look at how to connect with nature, including playing a fun game that uses all five of your senses. There are also quests for you to complete as you go through the book . . .

THE FORAGER'S CHALLENGE

Foragers, assemble – it's time for the ultimate foraging mission! Every plant and tree in this book (apart from the poisonous ones!) features two quests, which you can complete to earn Knowledge Points.

1. The Location Challenges: Gotta find 'em all!

These quests are easy. Simply find a real-life example of every plant and tree in this book.

2. The Special Challenges: The master forager

These quests will test your foraging skills, teach you fun and practical recipes, turn you into a master herbalist and engage all your senses.

There are 68 challenges in total, and you can earn one Knowledge Point for each of them. Jot down your points on page 215 as you complete each of the quests.

If you score . . .

0–10 POINTS

House Mouse Your foraging skills tend to lead you to the fridge.

11–20 POINTS

Field Mouse Your foraging skills are good enough to provide you with an outside snack.

21–30 POINTS

Squirrel Your foraging knowledge is fair; you can tumble through the countryside collecting wild food as you go.

31–40 POINTS

Hedgehog You've got a skilful foraging eye.

41–50 POINTS

Badger Your foraging knowledge is now so advanced that you can officially forage enough food to keep you full for ages!

51–60 POINTS

Fox You are a seasoned forager – there's not much you don't know about the wild.

61+ POINTS

Gold Crest You are now a true foraging master.

WHY FORAGE?

Learning to forage with friends and family means we can spend time together in nature, disconnecting from technology and reconnecting with each other. What's more . . .

Nature is good for us

Spending time outdoors can help reduce stress and anxiety, improves our mood and makes us happy!

It's physically healthy

Hiking up hills, wandering through woodlands and marching across meadows gets our hearts pumping. Being out in the open air and natural light is also really good for our brains and lungs.

It's nutritious and delicious

Talk about organic – wild food is as organic as it gets! What's more, many wild plants are more nutritious than the vegetables you'd buy in the shops. For instance, did you know that, by weight, stinging nettles contain more than four times the amount of calcium (great for our bones) than broccoli or spinach? (You just have to make sure the stinging nettles are cooked first . . .)

It teaches us the joys of seasonal eating

Foraging revolves around the seasons, so there's always something different to look out for and try. As the sun starts to shine in spring, wild garlic, tender young nettles and glorious dandelions appear, just calling out to be picked and eaten. The long days and increased warmth of summer bring a bounty of beautiful flowers and sweet fruits – nature's version of pick and mix! As autumn rolls round, nuts, apples and blackberries (and loads of other edible treats) are abundant, ready to be made into delicious crumbles or stored for winter.

It's super sustainable

Wild food has a very low carbon footprint, meaning it's great for the planet. It hasn't been picked miles away, wrapped in plastic and transported to supermarkets, and it doesn't require loads of pesticides or water for it to grow. Even better, it provides vital food and shelter for insects and wild animals, whether that's the pollen in flowers or the ripe fruits that appear later in the season.

THE TEN FORAGING COMMANDMENTS

1. If in ANY doubt, don't eat it!

Always check that you are 100 per cent certain that you have correctly identified a plant or tree before eating any part of it. Ninety-nine per cent sure isn't enough! Correct identification is vital in foraging, and it's always better to be safe than sorry. As you start on your foraging journey, if you think you know what a plant is, check that it matches our description and the photos in this book, and ask a trusted adult for a second opinion. Check the section on Poisonous Plants very carefully for more information (see page 188)

When trying foraged foods for the first time, it's also important to only eat a small amount at first. This is to ensure it agrees with you, and doesn't make you poorly!

We haven't covered fungus (which includes mushrooms) in this book, because it's too risky if you get it wrong. You need a specialist guide and proper training to forage for fungi safely. We also haven't included members of the carrot family for the same reason (see page 192).

2. Forage sustainably

Make sure you are mindful of birds and bees and always leave enough behind for wildlife. An easy way to approach this is to use the **10 per cent rule**: if there are fewer than ten plants available, leave them all for the local wildlife. If there are more than ten, take only 10 per cent of what's growing. It's usually easy to collect food from lots of different places as you pass through open spaces on a woodland walk or in a town or city, so don't take loads from just one spot.

Take care of the environment by treading lightly, and make sure you give back to nature when you can. Plant trees, build some bird boxes or homes for bees, and when you collect a bunch of wild plants leave them in the garden for half an hour before cooking them, to let the bugs run free!

Education leads to conservation

When we gain the knowledge that comes with learning how to forage, we start to see the world differently. We no longer shrug if we see trees being cut down to make way for a new car park; instead, we mourn the loss of a tree that provided food for birds, butterflies and bees. By better understanding our natural world, we open our eyes to how important it really is. And what do we do for the things we know are important? We take care of them! What starts out as going for a nice walk to hunt for a tasty snack can lead to a lifetime of caring for our planet.

'In the end, we will conserve only what we love, we will love only what we understand and we will understand only what we are taught.'

Baba Dioum, forestry engineer, conservationist and environmentalist

3. Think about pollution

Pee, pollution and pesticides don't taste great, and they're not great for our health, either. Walk the extra mile to get the freshest plants, avoid foraging near busy roads, and don't collect low-growing plants on pathways that are popular with dog walkers.

In urban areas some plants are considered to be weeds or pests, and can be sprayed with pesticides (chemicals that kill them). Pesticides are harmful for people to consume. Ask your local council which pesticides they use, where they use them, and if they display signs warning people that they have been applied. Don't forage in graveyards as lead from old coffins can leach into the soil and be absorbed by plants.

4. Know the law

There are some rules and regulations that you need to know so you can avoid breaking the law. These can vary from country to country, but basically, you need to stay off private land. This should be clearly marked with a sign saying something like 'DO NOT ENTER, PRIVATE'. If in doubt, it's best to presume it is private. Public paths and byways are usually marked on a map, so check before you head out. You can also try to speak to the landowner.

In the UK, it is illegal to uproot (dig up) any wild plants without a landowner's permission, even on common land (land that's owned by a person or organization, but can usually still be used for activities, such as walking or climbing). You should also avoid foraging in special wildlife reserves called Sites of Special Scientific Interest. You don't want to accidentally damage these precious areas. **It's worth reading more about the laws where you live so you can be confident you aren't doing anything wrong.**

5. Stay safe around animals

Although they may seem cute and cuddly, you can potentially be kicked by a horse or badly hurt by a stampede of running cows. They might be big, but they're definitely not slow! In fact, cows can run at around 27 kilometres per hour (km/h), while humans on average can only run at 9.5 km/h. **Avoid getting too close to animals when crossing a field or walking by a river or canal.** Swans and geese can be very protective of their nests and will swim towards you in a way that clearly says 'GO AWAY!' if they feel under threat. It's always better to be safe and walk the long way round rather than finding yourself fleeing from a raging bull or grouchy goose.

6. Be aware of ticks and how to remove them

Ticks are small insects that can attach themselves to skin and may cause an infection from a nasty disease called **Lyme disease**. They are found in lots of different places, including grasslands, woodlands, salt marshes, beaches that have beach grass habitats, and anywhere near animals, such as deer, cows, sheep or horses. They are particularly common in the warmer months between spring and autumn. For this reason, **it's a good idea to wear sturdy boots and tuck your trousers into your socks when you go walking.**

You should also keep a tick removal tool in your bag in case you spot one on your skin while you're out. Check yourself (and your dog!) over when you get in from your trip. Ticks are quite small so you need to look and feel carefully for any small bumps, which may be reddish in colour, or a small, dark spot on your skin. If you find a tick attached to your skin, ask an adult to help you. It's important to get the whole tick off without leaving any parts attached.

If you get a circular rash around where the tick bit you, go to your GP as you may need medication to treat Lyme disease. Sometimes you can be bitten by a tick and not notice it, and only one in three people gets the rash that is a symptom of Lyme disease. So if you've been outdoors and have other symptoms of Lyme disease, such as tiredness, muscle pain, joint pain, headaches, high temperature, chills or a stiff neck, go to your doctor. Don't worry if you are bitten by a tick or think you might have symptoms of Lyme disease, as it can be treated by your GP. The sooner you get help, the sooner you will feel better.

7. Expand your knowledge

This book is packed with foraging-related information and plant identification tips, but it should not be your *only* guide. Bear in mind that each species of plant or tree you come across on your travels may vary in appearance to the ones in here – and there are loads we didn't have space to include! Variations in climate and habitat also affect what's available, and rules can also be very different in different countries. For instance, foraging in England is a bit different to foraging in Australia or the USA! (There are fewer crocodiles and alligators, for a start . . .) Take what you learn here, then add to your knowledge by looking at the websites of expert organizations such as the Botanical Society of Britain and Ireland, the Woodland Trust, and the Wildlife Trusts. You can also join a local group or visit your library.

8. Health and safety

Be aware of any allergies or health conditions you have that could be affected by touching or consuming wild foods, or even just being in areas where there's lots of pollen or stinging insects. If you suffer from hay fever, avoid going out on particularly high pollen count days. **Some plants should not be eaten if you take certain forms of medication, so if you take medication, check with a medical professional before consuming any wild foods.**

Check the weather conditions before you set out. Although you're less likely to go foraging when it's snowy or icy, summer storms can pose a threat in the form of lightning, heavy rain and high winds. For information about appropriate clothing, see page 21.

You need to be particularly careful around water (where the ground might be slippery, for instance), and make sure you're aware of what to do if you or a companion falls in a river or the sea (even if you're not planning to forage near water).

Thorns and stinging nettles. If you get a thorn stuck under your skin, run the affected area under warm water, and ask your adult for help removing it. For a stinging nettle sting that turns into a rash, try rubbing with a dock leaf. If it doesn't go away wash with warm, soapy water. Avoid scratching the area, and seek medical help if the rash worsens.

Plan your route and take a paper map if you're not familiar with the area. Mobile phone reception can be patchy in the countryside, so you can't always rely on online maps or route planners. Someone in the group should carry a fully charged phone regardless. **Be on the lookout for barbed wire and electric fences in areas where there is livestock.** If you've got a dog, be sure to keep it on a lead around livestock.

Safe hands. When foraging, it's easy to miss things that are hidden but might hurt you, such as bees on flowers, or sharp objects on the ground. A good way to avoid getting stung, bitten or cut is to always look at where you're putting your hands. Never place your hands where you can't see what you are putting them in or on.

9. Stay safe in the kitchen

You've arrived back home with baskets brimming with tasty goodies. Now it's time to prepare them for eating or drinking! **Adult supervision is ALWAYS required in the kitchen.** See page 22 for more guidance about making your foraging bounty into tasty foods.

10. Enjoy the journey!

Life's not about arriving at the destination; it's about enjoying the journey. If you walk for miles without finding what you set out for, don't be sad. Embrace the fact that by searching for it you got to spend the day outdoors, listening to the birds sing and the bees hum. Finding a bumper crop is just the foraged cherry on the cake of the experience . . .

A GUIDE TO FORAGING EQUIPMENT

Great news! You don't need lots of (or any!) fancy equipment when it comes to foraging. A few medium-sized, clean, plastic containers with secure lids (for example, ice-cream tubs) are ideal, not least because soft stuff such as berries and other fruits won't get crushed, and any leaking juice will be contained in the container, rather than going all over your bag. Wasps will also lose interest in your foraged goodies much more quickly once they're sealed away.

Speaking of juice and wasps, it's a great idea to carry some biodegradable wipes, re-usable wet wipes or a damp flannel in a tub. If you're going fruit foraging, these are useful for cleaning sticky hands and faces once you've finished picking (and eating).

Non-juicy things such as nuts, flowers and leaves can go in resealable food bags or a tote bag – whatever is light and to hand.

The only other equipment we use for foraging is gloves for protection against stings and thorns, and a pair of scissors for cutting things cleanly (always ask your adult for help with this). We carry all of this in backpacks – one for each family member, to spread the load.

Don't forget to take along some water and snacks if you're going out for a longish walk. Hopefully you might be able to graze on some foraged treats (remember to wash anything you find before you eat it!), but you don't want to go hungry if you don't find anything.

It's also sensible to carry a mini first-aid kit containing plasters in case someone gets blisters or is swiped by a bramble, antiseptic cream and some bite and sting cream.

OUTDOOR ESSENTIALS

- Clean containers with secure lids
- Resealable food bags or a tote bag
- Gloves
- Pair of scissors
- Water and snacks
- Biodegradable wipes, reusable wet wipes or a damp flannel
- Mini first aid kit
- Mobile phone (in case of emergency)
- Hat and a long-sleeved top

There's no such thing as bad weather, just bad clothing

What you wear depends on the weather and where you're heading. A good pair of shoes, boots or wellies and decent socks make long walks more comfortable, keep feet cool in the summer or let you stomp through muddy puddles in wet weather.

Thicker trousers, such as jeans, and long sleeves protect the legs and arms from stings, scratches and insect bites. A hooded jumper can also come in handy when walking through stinging nettles, cobweb-filled woodlands or during a surprise attack of bad weather. We always wear a jumper or long-sleeved shirt, even on hotter days – they protect you from the sun, too. Hats are important for long walks in the sunshine to prevent sunstroke and sunburn. They look pretty cool, too! Make sure you apply suncream if it looks like a sunny day, and if it's an absolute scorcher consider heading outside when it's a little cooler. In cool or rainy weather, you'll also need a waterproof coat.

HINTS AND TIPS FOR
THE CHEFS

The most important thing to remember when cooking food is that you must have a adult with you at all times. This is particularly crucial when it comes to using ovens and hobs. Generally, it is just handy to have another person with you in the kitchen – you absolutely mustn't leave pans unattended, for instance, so having a chef partner to look after things is essential.

The equipment you need when turning your foraged goodies into even tastier food will vary depending on the food you've collected and the recipe you're using. Some things such as berries and nuts just need a wash before you tuck in, but others need to be chopped or cooked in some way.

Foraged foods will all need a rinse at the very least. Ensure you do so with cold running water. A colander is useful for this, so you don't lose any of your goodies! Make sure you also wash your hands before you start any cooking.

Knives, chopping boards, pans, wooden spoons and baking trays are fairly standard things you'll likely already have, but some recipes need slightly more specialist kit, such as a sugar thermometer, thick bottles for cordials, and jars for jams, pickles and soothing balms. A nutcracker might be handy for breaking into hard shells and getting to the good stuff. All of these are readily available, and you can often just reuse cleaned bottles and jars that once contained bought drinks and food.

Any homemade foods are best stored in a jar with a lid. If you're keeping food in the fridge or freezer, the jar needs a wash and a rinse before use. If storing at room temperature, you should wash the jar and sterilize it in the oven on a low heat. We show you how to do all of this in the jam recipe on page 54.

If you make drinks such as cordials, it's wise to **remove the lids every day, to release any build-up of air pressure.** Sometimes fermentation can occur in bottles, which is fine as long as the pressure doesn't build to the point the bottle explodes! You can also use **clip-top bottles**, which are easier to remove.

HOW TO MAKE A FRESHLY
FORAGED TEA

Herbal tea is a wonderful thing. It's a nice warm drink we can make for free, either when out in the fresh air or at home. Some taste like fruits and flowers, and others change colours! Many have health benefits, too.

Before you get stuck into the world of foraging, we thought we'd tell you how to make herbal tea, so you can try it for yourself. It's really easy. You only need a couple of things:

1. Hot water

Flasks these days are pretty awesome and keep water hot all day long. Pack a bottle of freshly boiled water into your backpack – just be sure to **ask an adult** to help you fill it up!

2. Foraged ingredients

Herbal teas are usually made with leaves, flowers, roots or fruits. These are then left in the hot water, to stew and infuse it – which means the water begins to taste a bit like the leaves or flowers you've added. The general rule of thumb is that you need to add around 2 teaspoons (tsp) of whatever ingredient you have to 1 cup of water and leave it in the water for around 5 minutes. **Make sure you've also washed your foraged ingredients before you use them.**

3. A sweetener

Some people enjoy herbal teas as they are, but others prefer a sweeter flavour. If you'd like a sweeter tea, add a little bit of homemade syrup (you can find out how to make these on pages 111 and 128).

4. A nice cup

You'll need something to drink your tea from! Any heatproof cup will do but a clear
one is best if you want to see the colours changing and flowers swirling like a little
floral tornado.

As you learn how to forage, experiment with herbal teas. Mix plants together to make
your own unique blends, and then add in different combinations of homemade
syrups. Elderflower tea is nice on its own, but what happens if you add some mallow
flowers or even some dandelion syrup?

There's an endless list of herbal tea colour and flavour possibilities. Here are some of
our favourites:

- Nettle (ensure the nettle leaves are in hot water for at least 10 seconds)
- Sweet violet flowers
- Elderflower
- Pineapple weed
- Strawberry leaf

A final note on our recipes.

For ingredient measurements we tend to use something called cups. It's
how we've always measured out our foods. Some of you (and your adults)
may be more familiar with grams and millilitres, so we've included a
conversion chart in the back of this book, on page 216, to help you make our
recipes, and avoid any confusion!

HOW LIVING THINGS ARE NAMED

You may notice as you read through this book that plants (and animals) can have more than one name. There's the familiar ones we use all the time – rose, beech tree, squirrel – and a more complicated-looking one in slopy writing called *italics*. Some also have lots of different everyday or **common names** (we call them **nicknames**), just to make things more confusing!

Scientists use something called **biological classification** to place living things (called **organisms**) into different categories, based on features that they do or don't share. It's all quite complicated, but all you need to know is that the **scientific name** for a living thing is usually made up of two words.

The first word is the name of the **genus** the species belongs to, and the second word is the **species**. A species is a group of organisms that are very similar, and capable of interbreeding – humans are a species! Whereas a genus is a group of one or more similar species. (You'll also see us talk about plants or flowers being related, and from the same **family** – a family is a much larger group that contains one or more genus.) This means that two related organisms can have the same first word (they belong to the same genus), but a different second word (they are different species). An example of this is the raspberry, *Rubus idaeus*, and the bramble, *Rubus fruticosus*.

This is not something to worry about – nobody is going to test you on it! – but it's interesting to know how scientists use these names to clearly identify and distinguish all living organisms. It means there is no confusion, and that all scientists use the same names, no matter what language they speak. Pretty cool, right?!

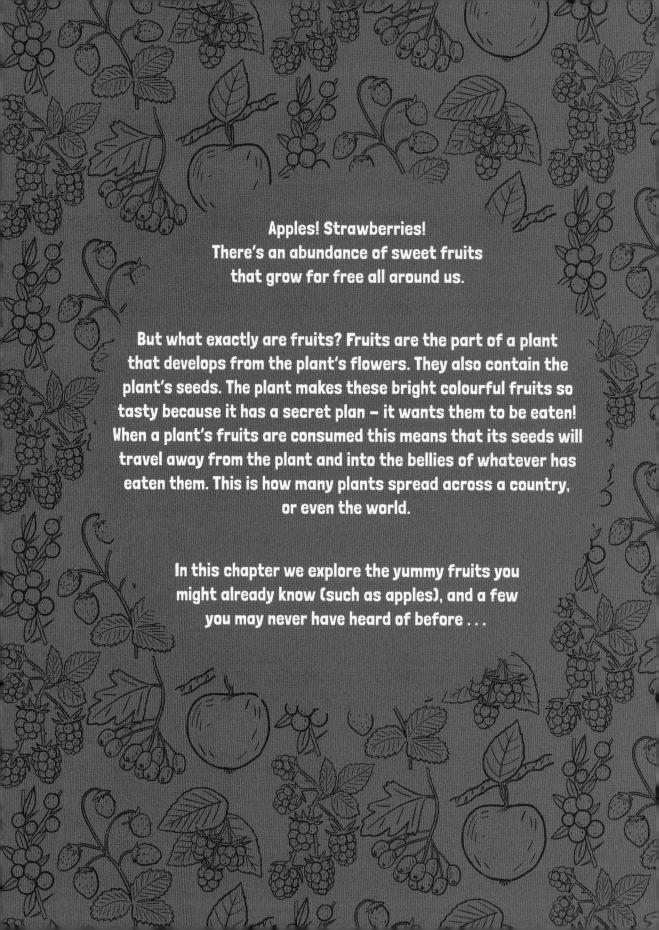

Apples! Strawberries!
There's an abundance of sweet fruits
that grow for free all around us.

But what exactly are fruits? Fruits are the part of a plant
that develops from the plant's flowers. They also contain the
plant's seeds. The plant makes these bright colourful fruits so
tasty because it has a secret plan – it wants them to be eaten!
When a plant's fruits are consumed this means that its seeds will
travel away from the plant and into the bellies of whatever has
eaten them. This is how many plants spread across a country,
or even the world.

In this chapter we explore the yummy fruits you
might already know (such as apples), and a few
you may never have heard of before . . .

FRUITS AND BERRIES

APPLE TREE

WHAT DOES IT LOOK LIKE? Though apple trees can look like a lot of other trees, there are ways of identifying them. They can grow to around 10 metres (m) tall, and their leaves tend to be an oval shape with toothed edges, which can grow from 3 to 10 centimetres (cm) in length. The flower blossoms have five petals, which may be white, pink or red in colour. These blossoms have a lovely sweet apple scent. The apples which grow from these blossoms can be green, yellow or sometimes a mix of colours with a shade of red.

WHERE DOES IT GROW? Apple trees can be found growing in hedgerows, woodlands, scrublands (land covered with low trees or bushes), towns and gardens.

SCIENTIFIC NAME *Malus domestica*

HOW LONG DOES IT LIVE FOR? Apple trees tend to live for around 30 to 100 years. It can take up to ten years for an apple tree to produce apples!

PARTS YOU CAN EAT Apples and blossoms

BEST TIME TO PICK IT You can snack on the fresh blossoms in spring or grab an apple in the summer and autumn. Try visiting an apple tree in the spring and take a good look at the apple blossom. Then return to this same tree each month and watch how the blossom slowly transforms into an apple!

THE FORAGER'S DICTIONARY

TOOTHED EDGES

When a leaf is described as having toothed edges this means that the ends of the leaf have little notches along them, creating a bumpy, tooth-like edge.

I DIDN'T KNOW THAT!

THOUSANDS OF APPLES

Did you know that there are more than 7,500 different types of apple in the world? Each one has its own unique flavour!

CRISPS

Apples can be made into crisps! More commonly known as apple snaps, these tasty treats can be popped into a lunch box and taken on your next foraging walk. We show you how to make these on page 32.

APPLE SEEDS CONTAIN CYANIDE!

Cyanide is a poison, which can actually be found in apple seeds. But don't worry, the seeds contain a *very* small amount of cyanide.

WHAT CAN YOU DO WITH IT?
Eat it!

Nothing beats a fresh, crisp apple, straight from the tree (washed first, of course!). They are delicious and nutritious and taste even better than the ones bought in a supermarket. The blossom tastes great too. Try placing a blossom petal in your mouth, and you might even get a faint taste of apples!

HOW MANY APPLES ARE IN AN APPLE? You can easily count the seeds in an apple, but can you count the apples in each seed? We can't ever know the true number, but here's a fun way of trying to work it out:

- An apple normally contains five to eight seeds.
- A single seed will grow into one apple tree.
- A tree will normally produce around 300 apples a year.
- So over the course of ten years, the tree produces 3,000 apples.
- Multiply 5 by 3,000 and each apple contains 15,000 apples over ten years!

FORAGER'S CHALLENGE

1. Find and identify an apple tree.

2. Make some apple snaps (see page 32).

'AN APPLE A DAY KEEPS THE DOCTOR AWAY!'

You've probably heard the grown-ups in your life say this before. (Another saying is 'an apple a day keeps anyone away if you throw it hard enough!' – but let's not start throwing apples, as it's a bit dangerous and they are far too valuable to waste!)

People love apples so much that they are now one of the most popular fruits around the world. But our love for apples isn't something new. Archaeologists have even found evidence that people have been eating apples since 6,500 BCE (8,500 years ago!).

Today we tend to just see apples as a healthy snack, but our ancestors saw apples as food and medicine. When you dive into the herbal history books, you'll find that apple juice might have been used as one of the earliest antidepressants, which meant it was given to people to help them feel happier. In the modern world, we see food and medicine as being two different things, but we are starting to understand more and more that what we eat affects not just our physical health, but may also affect how we feel.

Apples do indeed have lots of health benefits. They are rich in **pectin**, which is a fibre that feeds the good bacteria in our gut and means we can digest our food more easily. Some scientists call the gut our 'second brain', because it affects how we think – so apples really can create a healthy mind as well as a healthy body!

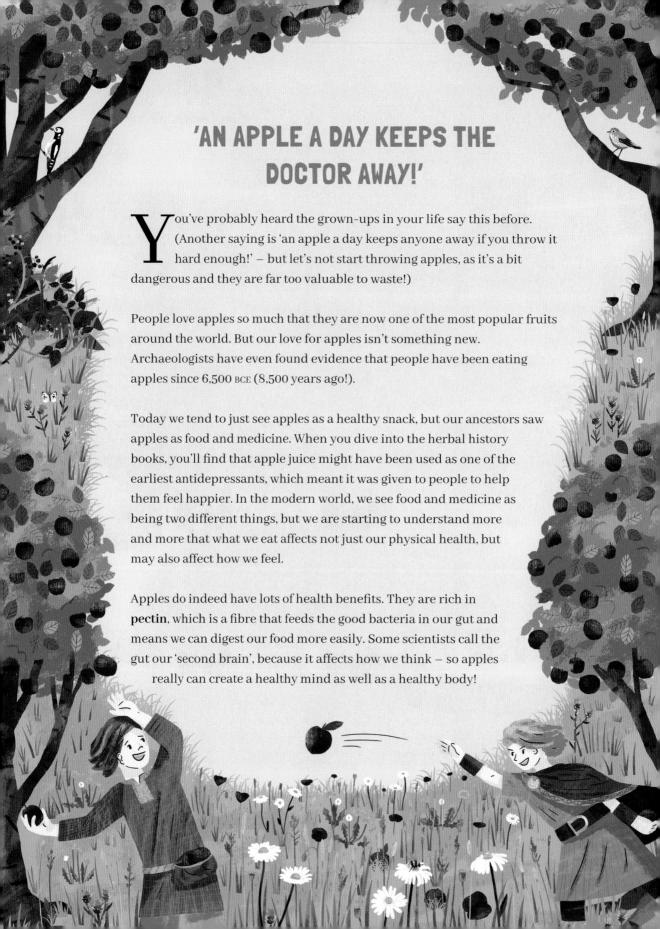

CATCH THAT APPLE!

The fact that apples are so delicious and abundant means they've had great importance throughout history. For some of our ancestors, they were even a bit magical.

The Vikings believed in a goddess called Idun. It was said that she gave apples to all the gods to make sure they stayed young forever. We also know apples were important to the Vikings, because one day archaeologists uncovered a buried Viking ship and guess what they found inside it? That's right – loads of apples!

The ancient Greeks believed Hercules (you've probably heard of him – famous for being incredibly strong) was sent to pick golden apples off the Tree of Life. This was part of 12 challenges set for him by a mythical ruler called King Eurystheus.

The ancient Greeks also used to throw apples at people they loved. Confused? They believed that if you threw an apple at someone you fancied, and they caught it, it meant they loved you in return. Nothing says true love like being hit in the face by a flying apple!

An ancient folktale even says that if you throw the seeds of your apple into a fire while saying the name of the person you love, and the seeds pop loudly, then they love you in return.

APPLE RECIPES

APPLE SNAPS

The perfect way to turn your apples into healthy, tasty snacks.

EQUIPMENT

Knife **(and an adult to help!)**
Large bowl,
Baking tray lined with baking paper

INGREDIENTS

4 or 5 apples
1 lemon, juiced
1 tablespoon (tbsp) ground cinnamon (optional)

METHOD

1. Preheat your oven to 50 degrees Celsius (°C)/120 degrees Fahrenheit (°F).

2. Chop your apples into thin slices (about the thickness of a pound coin) and pop out the seeds.

3. Put your apple slices in a bowl of water and squeeze in the lemon juice. (The lemon keeps the apple slices looking fresh. You can skip this step if you don't mind your apples turning brown! It's totally up to you.)

4. Leave the apples in the lemony water for half an hour.

5. Pour away the water then add your apple slices to the baking tray and sprinkle on the cinnamon (if you like the flavour!).

6. **Make sure you get an adult to help you with this bit!** Put your tray of apples in the oven and leave the door ajar (this lets the moisture escape and helps your apple slices to dry).

7. Bake for 1 hour, then turn the apples over and bake for a further 3 hours. Your apple slices will keep in an airtight container for at least two weeks. Just be sure to wash and rinse the container before use.

If you just can't wait three hours and want to eat your apple crisps right away, just bake for one hour on each side and enjoy! They won't be as crispy, but will still taste delicious.

APPLE SAUCE

Apple sauce is a great way to enjoy and preserve apples, and makes a fantastic addition to a roast dinner.

EQUIPMENT

Large saucepan
Potato masher

INGREDIENTS

8 apples, peeled and cored
1 cup water
2 tbsp brown or white sugar

METHOD

1. Put the peeled apples into the saucepan and add the water.

2. Bring to the boil. Once the water is boiling, reduce the heat and simmer for around 25 minutes, until the apples are soft. Stir occasionally.

3. Mash the apples with a potato masher, and add the sugar.

4. Keep simmering and mashing until the sauce is the consistency that you like it.

5. Enjoy! This sauce should be kept in a washed, airtight container in the fridge, where it will keep for up to a week, or it can be frozen if you want to keep it for longer.

WILD STRAWBERRY

WHAT DOES IT LOOK LIKE? The wild strawberry plant normally grows low to the ground, though they can reach up to around 30 cm in height. Their leaves grow in threes and have jagged edges. The flowers have five bright white petals, and the stem is a shade of green, or sometimes red. The fruit is much smaller than the strawberries you might buy from the shops. They are normally bright red and covered in tiny seeds, and they all have a little green hat on!

WHERE DOES IT GROW? Because they are so small, you can walk past wild strawberries without even knowing it. But keep your eyes wide open as you forage, and you might find them growing in open scrubland or open woodlands.

SCIENTIFIC NAME *Fragaria vesca*

NICKNAMES Woodland strawberry, alpine strawberry, Carpathian strawberry

PARTS YOU CAN EAT Just about all of it! The leaves, the flowers and, of course, the strawberries.

BEST TIME TO PICK IT The leaves are freshest and tastiest in spring, and the strawberries turn ripe, red and ready to eat in summer.

THE FORAGER'S DICTIONARY
RUNNERS

You might not think it from looking at them, but plants move around all the time. In fact, strawberry plants are known as runners. Now, this doesn't mean they can run away from you! It means they are a type of plant that can reach out with their stems, much like little arms. These burrow into the ground, and from them grow more strawberry plants, called **daughters**. If you grow a strawberry plant at home, it might have its own daughters, and strawberries will pop up all around your garden!

WHAT CAN YOU DO WITH IT?

Eat them!

You can use wild strawberries in all the same ways you'd use the strawberries you get from the market or supermarket. They can be turned into tasty things such as jams, smoothies or fruit salads; or, because of their small size, we love to enjoy them as a fresh snack while out and about – if we're lucky enough to find some and have water available so we can wash them first!

Strawberry tea that's wild and free

The leaves and flowers of wild strawberries can be dried and made into a delicious herbal tea. This tea has been drunk for thousands of years all around the world.

⚠ Strawberry leaves can be confused with other plants. First get to know strawberries in late spring and summer as they are easier to recognise when they are flowering and fruiting. Come back the following spring for fresh leaves when you are more familiar with them, and know where they grow.

I DIDN'T KNOW THAT!

ROLL UP! ROLL UP!

Have you ever wondered why a strawberry is called a strawberry? Over the years there have been many theories as to where the name started, but there's a chance it began hundreds of years ago, when children used to pick the fruits and sell them at market. The kids would string them along blades of straw, which they'd sell as **straws of berries** – hence the name!

ARE YOU MOCKING ME?

There's a berry that looks similar to the wild strawberry, called the **mock strawberry**. These lookalikes are nothing to worry about – they are safe to eat, though, sadly for us, they don't have much flavour. It's easy to tell the difference between wild strawberries and mock strawberries because wild strawberries have a typical strawberry shape, while mock strawberries look like little round balls. The mock strawberry flowers are yellow, while the wild strawberry flowers are white.

FORAGER'S CHALLENGE

1. Find and identify some wild strawberries.

2. Try stringing some wild strawberries across a blade of straw – just like they did hundreds of years ago!

FIT FOR AN EMPEROR

We all know strawberries are delicious and good for you. But throughout history, strawberries were also thought to have healing powers. People believed strawberry tea could help with sore mouths, sore throats and many other ailments. Some people even reckoned that the fruit, if squished over your teeth, would make them whiter!

In ancient Chinese mythology, the Yellow Emperor was a Chinese ruler, said to have lived over 4,000 years ago. Many believe he was the inventor of the wheel, armour, weapons, and also music. In some stories, he is well known for drinking strawberry tea, which he thought would stop his body ageing too quickly. Whatever the truth, we reckon if the gods were to drink anything, they'd probably drink strawberry tea!

LOVE IS IN THE AIR

Have you noticed how, if a TV programme or advert wants to show that people are in love, they might be shown eating strawberries together? This is an easy way of telling the viewer that love is in the air! But why is this the case? Why do strawberries represent love?

It's probably because stories and legends have always portrayed strawberries as something a bit magical. One particular myth says that if you break a double strawberry (two strawberries that have grown into one) in half and share it with someone else, then you would both fall head over heels in love.

And there are many other examples of this throughout history. In the UK, before chocolate had been introduced to Europe, strawberries were probably seen as the ultimate sweet treat. They were also viewed as a symbol of perfection, and stonemasons would carve them into altars and around the tops of pillars in churches and cathedrals. Next time you walk past a very old building – look up. You might just see a strawberry carved into the stone above you.

BRAMBLE

WHAT DOES IT LOOK LIKE? Bramble bushes grow in all directions – a bit like a giant, many-armed octopus! They can grow to around 4 m in height, and their leaves are oval-shaped with a jagged edge. They grow in groups of around six.

Their flowers are either white or a light shade of pink, and tend to have five petals. The blackberry fruits are a dark purple colour, appearing almost back. These berries are made of many little **drupelets**, which give them a bubbly appearance. The branches have painfully sharp thorns, which can grow to be very dense and are mightily strong!

WHERE DOES IT GROW? Lots of places, and all over the world! Woodlands, scrublands, towns and gardens, pathways, riversides, hedgerows and wastelands.

SCIENTIFIC NAME *Rubus fruticosus*

NICKNAMES Brambles, blackberry bush, black heg, wild blackberry, goutberry

PARTS YOU CAN EAT Leaves (when they are not fully grown), and the blackberries, of course!

THE FORAGER'S DICTIONARY

DRUPELETS

Drupelets are the little bobbles you find on fruit such as blackberries or raspberries. The name comes from the word drupe, which is a fleshy fruit with thin skin and a central stone containing the seed. For example, a plum, cherry, almond or olive.

BEST TIME TO PICK IT   The bramble's leaves are only nice to eat when they're fresh and young, which happens in early spring. You can tell when the leaves are fresh because they are small, light green and soft. They have a kind of nutty flavour, and make a great herbal tea. The blackberries are ripe and ready in the summertime.

WHAT CAN YOU DO WITH IT?

Eat them!

Blackberries are so good for you. They are packed full of vitamins A, C, E, K, B1, B2, B3, B9, calcium, iron, copper, magnesium, phosphorus, potassium and sodium. These are all essential for general good health.

Jams and pies

When it comes to turning blackberries into yummy food, we're not sure where to start. There's the classic blackberry jam, which is a great way to preserve all those blackberries (it tastes good, too!). Then we have blackberry pie, blackberry pudding, blackberry vinegar, blackberry ketchup and blackberry fruit roll-ups!

Check page 23 for tips about making herbal tea!

I DIDN'T KNOW THAT!

FOOD FOR THOUGHT

Brambles provide an abundance of food and shelter for wildlife. In the UK, 150 different species of insects, as well as many other animals, visit the bramble bush for their dinner. Everything from moths, caterpillars, bees, butterflies, beetles, birds, mice and more benefit from the food it provides.

FOOD FOR THE BRAMBLE BUSH?

Have you ever been snagged by a bramble bush? It's like it doesn't want to let you go, right? Perhaps the bramble thorns are out to catch you! We heard an amazing story from one shepherd: he loses sheep each year when they become entangled in brambles and die (poor things!). The sheep decompose, and their bodies apparently feed the bramble bush for years to come.

FORAGER'S CHALLENGE

1. Find and identify a bramble bush.

2. Make some blackberry leather (see page 43).

THE HISTORY OF THE BRAMBLE

The bramble bush has been here on Earth for a very long time. Archaeologists have found blackberries in the belly of a man who lived 7,000 years ago! Nobody truly knows where the bramble bush came from, and its origins are a mystery. But we do know that the bramble bush can be found in almost every corner of the globe, and has a long history of being used for food and medicine.

Throughout human history, the bramble bush has been used to treat a load of illnesses, especially for the stomach, skin and mouth. The blackberry leaves were even once thought to help with snake bites – at least that is what the ancient Greek doctor, Dioscorides, believed, way back in the year 90 CE!

Bramble leaf tea is also said to help soothe a cold. Another ancient Greek doctor, Hippocrates, even recommended people should soak the blackberry stems and leaves in white wine to help them during childbirth.

THE DEVIL'S REVENGE

There are a lot of historical myths, legends and superstitions associated with the bramble. One legend says that passing under an archway formed of bramble branches would cure and prevent many different diseases and illnesses. (This would apparently even work on cows. Can you imagine how difficult it would be to drag a poorly cow through a bramble archway!?)

But by far the most widespread superstition is that you should never eat blackberries after what's known as **Michaelmas Day**. Michaelmas Day used to be on 10 October, which is supposedly the day that Lucifer (also known as the Devil or Satan) was cast out of heaven. So between that day and the end of the calendar year (31 December) the blackberries should not be picked. And here's why . . .

The story goes that when Lucifer was cast out of heaven and fell to Earth, he landed in a sharp, thorny blackberry bush. Enraged by the pain caused by the sharp thorny brambles, he cursed it, vowing revenge.

It is said that Lucifer returns each year to seek his revenge on the brambles by making the blackberries unfit to eat. Some say he steps on them, others think he spits on them, there's even rumours he pees on them! And different versions of the story go even further, stating that if you eat blackberries after Michaelmas Day, you will die before the year is over . . .

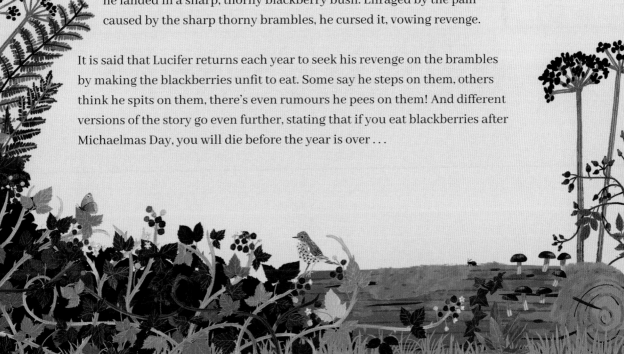

BLACKBERRY RECIPES

BLACKBERRY AND APPLE CRUMBLE

This classic dessert recipe is a great way to enjoy blackberries and apples!

EQUIPMENT

Medium-sized saucepan
Mixing bowl
Deep oven-proof dish

INGREDIENTS

4 or 5 apples, peeled, cored and chopped
    into small chunks
3–4 cups blackberries
1 cup sugar
1 tbsp cinnamon (optional)
2 cups plain flour
1 cup plant-based margarine or butter

Caution! The filling will be super hot straight out of the oven, so make sure you leave it to cool.

METHOD

1. Preheat your oven to 180 °C/350 °F.

2. Put the apple chunks and blackberries into the saucepan.

3. Add half the sugar to the pan with the cinnamon (if using). Mix it all up.

4. Pop your pan on a high heat and cook the fruit for about 5 minutes, or until it is soft.

5. For the crumble, add the plain flour to your mixing bowl, along with the margarine or butter. Mix together using your hands (don't worry, it's OK if it gets messy!), then add the rest of the sugar. You should end up with a mixture that has a breadcrumb-like consistency.

6. Pop your apple and blackberry mix in the oven-proof dish, then add your crumble mix on top of this. Make sure it covers the edges on the dish.

7. Bake for 45 minutes until golden brown.

BLACKBERRY LEATHER

What we now call a fruit roll-up is actually an ancient method of preserving fruit – which people used to call fruit leather.

EQUIPMENT

Blender or large mixing bowl
Baking tray lined with baking paper
Sieve (optional)
Sharp knife
Metal spoon

INGREDIENTS

50–60 blackberries
1 tsp honey or golden syrup (optional)

METHOD

1. Put your blackberries into a mixing bowl or blender. Add your honey or syrup if using. Blend (or use your hands if using a mixing bowl) to smush the blackberries into a smooth pulp.

2. Pour the pulp on to the middle of the baking tray (if you don't want seeds in your leather, push the pulp through a sieve, which you can place over the tray).

3. Use the back of a spoon to smooth out your pulp, spreading it to the edges of the tray.

4. Pop this into the oven at 50 °C/120 °F for 3–4 hours. Leave the oven door slightly open, and check on it every hour to ensure it's not burning.

5. You can check if your leather is done by feeling if there are any squidgy areas left – it should be totally solid. Once all of the squidge is gone, your leather is done! Remove from the oven and leave it to cool.

6. **Definitely get your nearby adult to do this next bit.** Cut around the edge of your leather to get rid of the crispy edges (as they don't roll very well!). While it's still on the baking paper, chop your leather into 3-cm wide strips, peel them away from the paper and roll them up into little rolls of blackberry leather.

If you can resist eating it all in the first week, your leather will last for at least six weeks in a sealed and washed jar.

HAWTHORN TREE

WHAT DOES IT LOOK LIKE? The hawthorn tree can grow to around 15 m tall. Its leaves are wonderfully unique because they have around six deep **lobes**, with each lobe bending in an alternate direction to the lobe that joins it. The leaves are also a darker shade of green on the top than on the bottom. The hawthorn flowers are white or sometimes pink, and each has five petals.

The hawthorn berries are a deep shade of red and look like tiny apples. The shade of red can vary from tree to tree – some are dark, while others are bright red. These berries, known as haws, each contain a single seed.

WHERE DOES IT GROW? Hawthorn trees are a common tree in the UK, and you'll find them growing in hedgerows, fields, pathways and woodlands.

SCIENTIFIC NAME *Crataegus monogyna*

NICKNAMES May tree, whitethorn, quickthorn

HOW LONG DOES IT LIVE FOR? Around 250 to 400 years

PARTS YOU CAN EAT Leaves, flowers and berries. When you squash open the haw berry, it has an oily texture and tastes like a slightly overripe apple.

BEST TIME TO PICK IT You can eat the fresh leaves and blossoms in early spring. The haw berries are ready to eat when they turn red, which is usually in the autumn.

THE FORAGER'S DICTIONARY

LOBES

When a leaf is described as having lobes, it means it has parts that bulge or stick out. These lobes can be either rounded or pointed.

WHAT CAN YOU DO WITH IT?

A fresh snack

When the hawthorn leaves are fresh, they make a nice savoury-flavoured snack. In the olden days, children would snack on these leaves and – for some reason – refer to them as bread and cheese! This is maybe because the leaves have a nutty flavour, like some cheeses.

Mini apples

The haw berries both look and taste like apples! These little berries are full of antioxidants, which are great for our bodies, and means the berries are an excellent healthy snack. Make sure you DO NOT eat the seeds, though, as these aren't edible.

Hawthorn Ketchup

Yes, that's right, hawthorn can be made into ketchup! This delicious sauce doesn't just have to be made from tomatoes – haw berries actually make an amazing ketchup alternative, and it tastes great on home-baked chips.

I DIDN'T KNOW THAT!

A SIGN OF SUMMER

When the hawthorn flowers, it tells us that summer is on its way!

THE BLACK DEATH

The bubonic plague (also known as the Black Death) was an infection that spread across Europe from 1347 to 1351, returning in the 1600s, causing the death of millions. People who lived through these times thought that the hawthorn blossoms somehow smelled like the Black Death, which led many to believe that the hawthorn tree was linked somehow with death itself.

We now know that hawthorn flowers produce a chemical called **trimethylamine**, which is one of the first chemicals produced by a decomposing dead body. So there is a connection after all!

FORAGER'S CHALLENGE

1. Find and identify a hawthorn tree.

2. Try a hawthorn berry – and see if you can taste a hint of apple! (Just make sure to spit out the seed.)

HAW IS WHERE THE HEART IS

It was once believed that the hawthorn tree, and in particular the haw berries, helped us with one of the most important parts of our body: our heart! The leaves, flowers and berries were used to treat many heart-related illnesses over time, such as high blood pressure, heart palpitations and heart failure.

The hawthorn wasn't just used for healing hearts. Here is what famous ancient Greek physician Dioscorides, who was around in the first century CE, had to say about it:

It is said by some that drinking the seed of the hawthorn causes a woman to bring forth a male child.

We're pretty sure this one isn't true! But when modern science dived into the wonderful world of the hawthorn, it found that the berries contain properties that may help lower blood pressure, help treat atherosclerosis (clogged arteries) and even reduce anxiety.

FAIRIES UNDER THE TREE

The hawthorn is no stranger to folklore. It's surrounded by many superstitions, legends and tales. People used to believe (and some still do) that fairies live under the hawthorn tree and the tree itself is under fairy protection. Because of this, many thought that it was bad luck to cut down a hawthorn tree. (Well, cutting down a fairy's house probably isn't good luck, right?)

Fascinatingly, this superstition survives today. Next time you're walking through the countryside, keep your eye out for a hawthorn tree, and you'll notice that often it will be growing alone, maybe in the middle of a field. This is because when all the other trees in the field were chopped down, the hawthorn tree was left where it was, to avoid any bad luck!

WILD RASPBERRY

WHAT DOES IT LOOK LIKE? Wild raspberry plants are easy to identify because of their bright red, bubbly looking berries. These raspberries grow from red and green thorny branches. The plant has **compound** leaves with serrated edges that grow in clusters of five, six or seven. These leaves are green on top and usually a lighter shade of green underneath.

WHERE DOES IT GROW? Just like brambles, wild raspberries grow in lots of places, but are much harder to find! If you're lucky, you can spot them along pathways, hedgerows or even in open sunny woodlands.

SCIENTIFIC NAME *Rubus idaeus*

NICKNAMES Hindberry, raspis, European red raspberry.

PARTS YOU CAN EAT Leaves and raspberries.

BEST TIME TO PICK IT The raspberry leaves and fruits can be picked and eaten throughout summer and autumn.

WHAT CAN YOU DO WITH IT?

Eat it!
Raspberries are one of the most delicious fruits in the world. If you find some, consider it your lucky day and get stuck in.

Make sorbet
What's sorbet, you say? It's a frozen dessert made from iced fruit. Simply mash the raspberries and then freeze them to create a delicious raspberry dessert. Find out how to make your very own fruit sorbet on page 56.

THE FORAGER'S DICTIONARY

COMPOUND

When leaves are described as compound, it means that the leaf is formed from a number of smaller leaves all joined to one stem.

Make raspberry tea

Everyone knows you can eat raspberries, but you can also do special things with the leaves. Raspberry leaf tea is expensive to buy in the shops, but making your own is a cheap and fun alternative – and it tastes delicious!

Check page 23 for tips on making herbal tea!

I DIDN'T KNOW THAT!

A RAINBOW OF RASPBERRIES

Raspberries are bright red, right? But did you know that there are hundreds of different types of raspberry? And they come in many different shades of bright beautiful colours! You can get white, black, purple and even golden yellow raspberries!

FORAGER'S CHALLENGE

1. Find and identify a raspberry bush.

2. Try painting a picture using only raspberry juice!

ALL ABOARD THE RASPBERRY TRAIN

Scotland is famous for its delicious raspberries. During the 1950s, raspberries were transported from Scotland to London on a train called the *Raspberry Special*!

BLOW A RASPBERRY?

You probably know what it means to 'blow a raspberry'. This is because it's also the rather unfortunate noise we make when we eat a raspberry that's gone off (otherwise known as a fart!). So make sure the raspberries you eat are freshly picked!

FRUIT OF THE GODS

What does a mountain in Greece have to do with raspberries? Well, the story goes that the mountain was named after a nurse called Ida, who was tasked with looking after Zeus, head of all the Greek gods. Raspberries grew in abundance on this mountain – they were white though, not red. One day, Ida was picking these delicious white raspberries for Zeus, when she accidentally pricked her finger on a raspberry thorn! It is said that when her blood spilled over the white raspberries it stained the fruit red – and they've stayed that way ever since.

BLACKTHORN

WHAT DOES IT LOOK LIKE? The blackthorn grows to around 7 m tall – its bark is dark in colour, and in some lights can appear almost pitch black. In winter the tree can look a bit sad, but in early spring it suddenly bursts into life with bright **blossoms**, which are a bright shade of white with five petals. The leaves are small and oval-shaped with a toothed edge, and turn yellow and fall off in autumn.

By autumn, the blossoms of the blackthorn disappear, and in their place sloe berries arrive, which are dark black in colour, with a hint of blue.

WHERE DOES IT GROW? You'll find blackthorn trees growing in lots of countryside places, because they are popular for making hedges. You also find them growing in woodlands.

SCIENTIFIC NAME *Prunus spinosa*

NICKNAMES Sloe

HOW LONG DOES IT LIVE FOR? Blackthorns tend to live for around 100 years.

PARTS YOU CAN EAT The sloe berries. But beware – they are very sour!

BEST TIME TO PICK IT The sloe berries are ready to pick in the autumn.

THE FORAGER'S DICTIONARY

BLOSSOM

Blossom is often the flower of a stone fruit, which is part of a family of plants called Rosaceae (the rose family). As well as sloes this family includes cherries, apples and haws.

WHAT CAN YOU DO WITH IT?
Eat it (well, sort of!)

Sloes are pretty sour if eaten raw. But they are completely safe to eat, and it's fun to try anyway. Or you could get your friend to have a go and watch their face turn all scrunched!

A touch of frost

What's great about sloes is, after the first frosts of the year, they are less bitter. And if you cook sloes, they become much more delicious, and end up tasting a bit like plums. You could make them into a jam, or heat them up and cover them in melted chocolate!

I DIDN'T KNOW THAT!

THE DARK AGES

The blackthorn tree's bark becomes darker with age. It might even be how the tree got its name!

POISON THORNS

And the second part of its name? That comes from the fact that the tree's branches are covered in sharp thorns. Be careful around these, because if you get one stuck under your skin, it can cause what's known as blackthorn poisoning. This isn't deadly, but can create some nasty swelling, so be on your guard.

BLACKTHORN OR HAWTHORN?

The blackthorn and hawthorn look very similar, especially in winter and spring. You can tell the two trees apart in early spring because the blackthorn blossoms before the hawthorn.

FORAGER'S CHALLENGE

1. Find and identify a blackthorn tree.

2. Visit the same blackthorn tree in all four seasons to watch how the tree transforms throughout the year.

THE ICEMAN COMETH

For thousands of years, sloe berries were probably used for food and medicine. One of the reasons we think this is because sloe berries were discovered next to the medical kit of the oldest naturally mummified person ever found in Europe!

This person was given the name Ötzi the Iceman. Ötzi was a man aged about 45 who is thought to have died around 3,300 BCE – which means he was alive 5,300 years ago, making him older than the Egyptian pyramids and Stonehenge! Ötzi was accidentally discovered by hikers in 1991, in a glacier on the border between Austria and Italy.

He is 'naturally mummified' because, when he died, he was preserved in the ice of the glacier for thousands of years. His organs, the majority of his body tissue, fingernails, hair (even the lunch in his belly) was all frozen, and meant scientists could discover a huge amount about how humans lived all that time ago.

Also preserved was a medical kit used by Ötzi. Among other things, it contained a fungus called birch polypore and lying next to it was a single sloe berry. Scientific tests have shown that Ötzi wasn't a well man when he died. He had a parasite called whipworm and was suffering from Lyme disease. Although we can't be sure (because the sloe berry wasn't in the medical kit), it's believed that Ötzi was using the combination of sloe berries and birch polypore to help combat these infections.

ALL ABOUT ÖTZI

Here are some amazing facts that we've been able to find out about Ötzi . . .

- He had a gap-toothed smile.

- He wore clothes made from animal hides and owned tools that included a net for carrying things and a dagger with a tree-fibre sheath.

- He had a bow made out of yew tree and a copper axe.

- Not only was Ötzi rocking a load of cool kit, he also had tattoos! He currently holds the world record for the oldest tattoos ever found.

- Ötzi is so well preserved that we even know how he died. The poor man was murdered! He was most likely shot in the back with an arrow, then fell into the snow and ice, where he was frozen for thousands of years.

FRUIT TREATS

You can use any of the fruits and berries you've foraged in these delicious, yet simple, recipes . . .

JAM

Jam is a tasty, sweet treat and has been used as a way of preserving fruit for years. (Millions of years, in fact – jam goes back as far as the Stone Age!) Preserving means that the fruit stays good to eat for longer, and doesn't turn mouldy and rotten for ages. Jam is great to have on toast, or anything you want to make fruity and sweet, such as cakes and biscuits.

It's really easy to make homemade jam. For this recipe you could use strawberries, raspberries or blackberries – the pictures opposite show jam made using wild raspberries. The amount we've suggested below will make around three normal-sized jars of jam.

EQUIPMENT

Large mixing bowl
Large saucepan
Sieve (optional)
Jars (as many as you need, washed thoroughly and rinsed)

INGREDIENTS

500 grams (g) fruit
500 g caster sugar

METHOD

1. Squish up your fruit of choice in a large mixing bowl. You can do this with your hands, so don't be afraid to get messy.

2. Once your fruit is a pulp-like consistency, transfer it to the saucepan. If you don't want any large chunks or seeds in your jam, you can push it into the saucepan through a sieve.

3. Add the sugar to the saucepan, stir it into the fruit, then heat the mixture on a low heat and slowly bring it to the boil. Make sure you stir the mixture as you do this.

4. Once the mixture starts to bubble, boil for a further 4 minutes, stirring so it doesn't burn.

5. If you decide not to store your jam in the fridge, you'll need to sterilize your jars, to make sure they don't contain any germs. Put them in the oven, on a low heat (we recommend 50°C/120°F) for 5 minutes.

6. Being very careful (**use oven gloves and have your adult on hand to help you**), take the jars out of the oven, add an equal amount of jam to each jar and wait for it to cool before storing or eating it. This can last up to a year in or out of the fridge.

FRUIT SORBET

Sorbet (also known as water ice) is a refreshing food that is the perfect way to use the fruits you've foraged. Like jam, it also preserves the fruit, so it lasts for longer. It is an ideal cooling snack for a hot summer's day.

Again, you can use any fruits you want for this (the pictures here show us using raspberries), and it's really easy to make. You just need your fruit, a blender and some space in the freezer.

EQUIPMENT

Blender (and an adult who will help you with this!)
Freezer
Small bowls or ice-cream cones to serve

INGREDIENTS

Your fruit, chopped into bite-size pieces. This can be as much or as little as you want. As a general guide, 225 g of fruit makes one generous helping of sorbet.
1 tbsp syrup or honey (optional)

METHOD

1. Put your fruit in the freezer for a few hours, until it's frozen through.

2. **Your adult must help with this next step**. Take the fruit out of the freezer, add it to the blender (along with the syrup or honey if using) and blend until it has a smooth consistency.

3. Put the mixture in the freezer again for a few hours.

4. Once the mixture is solid, remove from the freezer and let it sit for five minutes.

5. Serve in bowls or on ice-cream cones, and enjoy!

A FINAL FRUIT FACT

What came first – the blossom or the apple?

Answer: the blossom! All fruits come from flowers,
so on an apple tree the blossom will appear first,
which will disappear when the apple comes along.
But not all flowers turn into fruits.

Plants and bushes cover the
countryside here in the UK.

But have you ever walked through nature and felt like
you were seeing the same plain green plants? This is
what's known as becoming 'plant blind'! The reality is we're
surrounded by diversity, from gorse bushes and plantain, to
pineapple weed and wild garlic. There's a whole world of
plants and bushes growing right outside our front doors.

All we have to do to see them is look a
little closer . . .

PLANTS AND BUSHES

GORSE

WHAT DOES IT LOOK LIKE? You'll find it difficult to miss a gorse bush! They can grow up to 4 m tall and are covered in dense, prickly leaves. But its bright yellow flowers give it a much more friendly feel, and if you lean in closely, you'll notice it has a wonderfully sunny, almost coconutty, smell. The flowers actually look a little like the ones that grow on pea plants, with black or brown **seed pods** covered in white hairs. There are three or four seeds per pod.

WHERE DOES IT GROW? Gorse is quite a tough bush and likes to grow in tough places where other plants might struggle. You'll most likely find it growing on scrublands, wastelands, heaths, coastal habitats or on mountains.

SCIENTIFIC NAME Gorse has a number of proper names! They are: *Ulex europaeus, Ulex gallii, Ulex minor*.

NICKNAMES Furze, whin, prickly broom

PARTS YOU CAN EAT The bright yellow gorse flowers, though it's not recommended to eat too many. Eat no more than 10 at a time, and only do so occasionally.

BEST TIME TO PICK IT You can find gorse flowers growing all year long. This is because three species of gorse actually grow in the UK. They look similar and flower at separate times, giving us gorse all year round.

WHAT CAN YOU DO WITH IT?
Gorse tea
Combining gorse flowers and hot water makes a delicious bright yellow cup of herbal tea. We recommend taking a flask and a clear cup with you next time you go on a long walk, so you can enjoy that bright yellow colour! Make sure to collect flowers that smell strongly of coconut to help give it that extra flavour.

THE FORAGER'S DICTIONARY
SEED POD

A seed pod is a part of a plant that acts like a sort of case, to hold a plant's seeds. Did you know that a pea is actually a type of plant seed? And when you buy fresh peas from the farmer's market, they are very often still in their pod. **Unlike peas, gorse seed pods can't be eaten, though!**

See page 23 for tips on making herbal tea!

Bright yellow dye

Because gorse flowers have such a wonderful yellow colour, they can be added to lots of different things to turn them bright yellow. They can change the colour of food, for instance, or even clothes (though don't try adding the flowers to your washing at home!).

THE BURNING ISSUE

Gorse is very flammable, which means it catches fire easily. It also burns to a very hot temperature, so a long time ago people used gorse as a fuel. In fact, burning gorse was so popular that in Oxfordshire it was made law that only a small amount of gorse could be used for fuel per day – just the amount a person could carry on their back. Can you imagine walking home with loads of spiky gorse on your back? Ouch!

ALIENS AT WORK

In 2005, a man named Dean got stuck in a thicket of gorse bushes. In fact, he was so stuck that he had to be airlifted out by helicopter! Dean ended up spending a full two days in the gorse thicket and can't actually remember how he ended up there. The rescue team who winched him to safety said: **'The man was in a patch of gorse bush ten feet deep! We have no idea how he got there. He was right in the middle of the gorse. It was like he had been dropped there by a spaceship. It was certainly one of our stranger rescues.'**

I DIDN'T KNOW THAT!

COCONUT OR ALMOND?

Some people say gorse smells of coconuts, others say almonds. It's tricky to know which one is right – some even say they give off the scent of vanilla. What we do know is that the gorse only begins to release its scent when it's been in the sunshine.

EXPLODING SEED PODS!

Gorse seed cases actually explode in hot weather, firing out thousands of seeds on to the ground. These then grow into new gorse bushes (some can even start growing 30 years after they reach the ground). If you listen very carefully on a hot day, you can sometimes hear the gorse bushes popping.

WHY CAN'T PEA BE FRIENDS?

Gorse bushes are in the Fabaceae family. This family also contains the pea plant, which means gorse is a relative of the peas we eat for dinner! Unlike peas, though, we can't eat the little gorse seeds.

WILDLIFE HEAVEN

Because gorse flowers in the colder months of the year, it provides food for many insects. Birds also love to nest in gorse, as its thick prickly habitat provides them with a safe place to live – a bit like being safe inside a spiky castle!

FORAGER'S CHALLENGE

1. Find and identify a gorse bush.
2. Smell your way through the gorse to find one with the sweet scent of coconuts.

HAPPY, HEALTHY GORSE

Gorse has been used throughout history to cheer people up. No one is quite sure how gorse was used to make people happier, though. Maybe a cup of bright yellow gorse tea brought someone joy, or perhaps a trip to collect gorse flowers could help brighten up a day!

Gorse was also used to treat jaundice, which is a condition where skin and eyes take on a yellow colour. Although there is no evidence that this ever actually worked.

A KISS FROM A GORSE

There's a popular saying about gorse that's still used today: *When gorse is out of bloom, kissing is out of fashion.* This suggests that kissing is never out of fashion because gorse bushes are always in flower!

HIDDEN WITCHES

Centuries ago, people believed that when the gorse was in full flower, it meant witches were hiding within it. We've heard one folktale say that on May Eve (30 April), witch hunters would set the gorse bush on fire in the hope of catching these witches, before they transformed themselves into hares to flee the flames.

CLEAVERS

WHAT DOES IT LOOK LIKE? A well-fed cleavers plant can grow to 6 m tall! The plant has a square-shaped stem, often with dark red lines running up the sides. If you look really closely, you can see the plant is covered in tiny hooked hairs, which can cling to clothes or animal fur – even when we don't want them to! Its leaves are lance-shaped (**lanceolate**) and grow in groups around the stem. In early summer, you may find cleavers produce very small white flowers with four petals. Towards the middle of summer, small sticky seed balls start to appear on the plant. These begin life a bright green colour, then fade to a reddish brown towards the end of summer, before becoming grey in the autumn.

WHERE DOES IT GROW? Cleavers is a crawling plant that clings to other plants as it grows. You'll most likely find it crawling through hedgerows, woodlands, gardens and urban areas.

SCIENTIFIC NAME *Galium aparine*

NICKNAMES Goosegrass, sticky weed, sticky willy, bedstraw

PARTS YOU CAN EAT Stem, leaves and seeds

BEST TIME TO PICK IT The stem and leaves are fresh in early spring.

THE FORAGER'S DICTIONARY

LANCEOLATE

When a leaf is described as lanceolate, it means it is shaped like the head of a lance. A lance is the end of a long spear, and in ancient times was used by warriors who rode on horseback.

WHAT CAN YOU DO WITH IT?
Pesto
You can eat cleavers as you find them. Sometimes they taste wonderfully fresh, and sometimes they can be a little bitter. But they're always tasty when blended into a fresh, bright green pesto. Find out how you can make your very own cleavers pesto on page 67.

What did the cleavers say to the chef? Stop pesto-ing me!

A pot herb
Cleavers is known as a pot herb. This means it's a herb that can be cooked in a pot and used to bulk up meals such as soups or stews. It goes nice and soft when boiled and absorbs flavour, so is a perfect addition to a piping hot bowl of soup.

I DIDN'T KNOW THAT!

RED IN TOOTH AND CLAW
Look again at those red lines on the stems of cleavers. That red colour flows up from the plant's roots and is a strong natural dye. Some even say it's so strong that when birds eat a lot of cleavers, it turns their bones red!

POOR MAN'S COFFEE
Cleavers is in the Rubiaceae family, which means it's closely related to the coffee plant, where we get coffee beans from. Caffeine is the substance in coffee beans that wakes people up when they drink it, and cleavers beans also contain a small amount of caffeine.
In late summer, when the seeds are ready to pick, it's possible to make a fresh cup of cleavers coffee.

FORAGER'S CHALLENGE
1. Find and identify a cleavers plant.
2. Cleavers are so sticky! Try sticking a cleavers plant to the back of someone you know and see how long it takes them to notice . . .

CLEANING THE MILK

Cleavers has been an important plant throughout human history. It appears much earlier in spring than many other plants, so it provided our ancestors with food after what had often been a long, difficult winter where nothing much grew. When cleavers began to grow, it meant that there was fresh food to eat – a sign that winter was coming to an end and spring was just around the corner.

People also believed that cleavers could cleanse their bodies after winter – that it could flush out toxins and make room for good health in spring and summer. And there may be some truth in this. For instance, scientists have found that the cleavers plant might be able to help with skin infections.

The cleavers' proper name, *Galium aparine*, comes from the Greek word for milk because cleavers were once used to 'clean' milk as it came from the cow. The hairy barbs on the cleavers stems would catch the hair and muck in the milk as it was poured through the plant.

CLEAVERS PESTO

Pesto is an amazing food, which can be mixed with pasta, spread on toast or used as a dip (we like using carrot sticks). The possibilities are endless!

Pesto is usually made from blended plants, with oils and nuts often added for extra flavour. For this recipe, we're going to use cleavers, which makes a highly nutritious and delicious pesto.

You can 'pesto' any plant you like, though, as long as it's edible, of course. Wild garlic also makes a fantastic pesto.

EQUIPMENT

Blender (used with help from your adult)

INGREDIENTS

2 cups of cleavers (bunched up). **Ensure these are freshly picked, undamaged (not crushed or wilting) and thoroughly washed.**
⅓ cup pine nuts
½ cup olive oil
2 cloves garlic, peeled and chopped
Pinch of salt

Because of its ingredients, pesto poses a small risk of botulism (a type of food poisoning) if not stored properly. This isn't anything to worry about! But you should only store it in the fridge, and for a maximum of five days. If freezing, it should be frozen immediately after being made, and eaten as soon as defrosted.

METHOD

1. **Get your adult to help with this first step!** Add the cleavers, pine nuts, olive oil, garlic and salt into the blender and blend until it forms a smooth consistency.

2. And hey pesto! Pesto should be kept in the fridge, and will last for four days, or several months if frozen. If kept in a sealed container, it's important that the container is washed, and that the pesto has a layer of oil on top, to avoid any mould forming.

RIBWORT PLANTAIN

WHAT DOES IT LOOK LIKE? Ribwort plantain has long lanceolate-shaped leaves (see page 64) that form a rosette (an intricate circle, see page 78) around the base of the plant. These leaves have long, deep veins running from the base of the leaf to the pointed tip. The leafless stem grows up from its rosette of leaves, with a flower at the top. The flower head is a greyish colour and has unique protruding white **stamens**.

WHERE DOES IT GROW? Plantain likes to grow in places where the soil is disturbed or squished down. This means it's actually very common in towns, gardens, along pathways or in open fields.

SCIENTIFIC NAME *Plantago lanceolata*

NICKNAMES Narrowleaf plantain, lamb's tongue, waybread

PARTS YOU CAN EAT Leaves, flower heads and seeds

THE FORAGER'S DICTIONARY

STAMEN

A stamen is the 'male' part of a flower and consists of a thin stem that holds an anther at its tip. The anther is the part of a flower that produces pollen, which is crucial in reproduction.

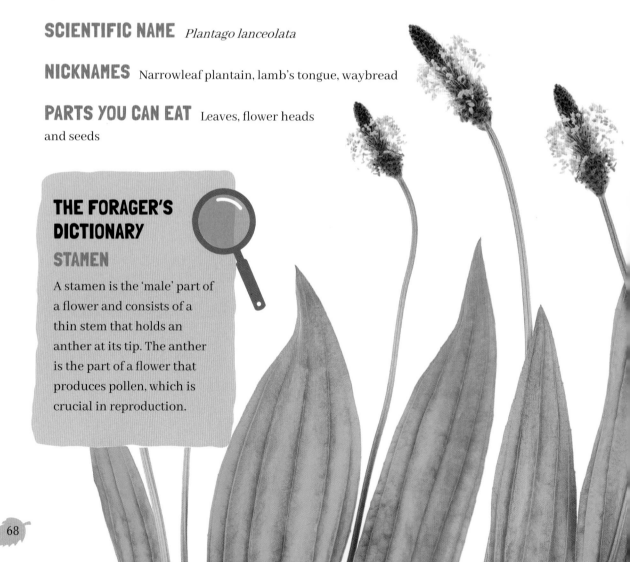

BEST TIME TO PICK IT You can find plantains all year long, but they are most abundant in spring and summer.

WHAT CAN YOU DO WITH IT?

Mushroom snacks

When you next come across plantain, give it a wash, and then take a bite out of one of the grey flowers. You'll notice it tastes exactly like a mushroom! Pick these flowers when they're young and fresh for a healthy snack when you're out and about.

Plantain soup

The leaves of the plantain are quite bitter when eaten fresh, which is why they're more commonly used as a pot herb and added to recipes such as soups and stews.

Added flavour

In the autumn, the plantain flower heads turn to brown seeds, which can be used in recipes. The seeds add the plantain's natural mushroom flavour to whatever it is you're cooking.

FORAGER'S CHALLENGE

1. Find and identify a ribwort plantain.

2. Try a fresh flower head and experience its mushroom-like flavour!

I DIDN'T KNOW THAT!

SOLE OF THE FOOT

A different species of plantain called *Plantago major* (known as Greater, or Broad-leaved Plantain) used to be called the 'white-man's footprint' by some Indigenous Peoples in North America, because it seemed to follow the European settlers around wherever they went. This happened because the plantain seeds got stuck to the bottom of the settlers' shoes. They would tread on the seeds in their own countries, then bring them to North America, squishing them into the ground, where they would grow into plantain. The scientific name for plantain, *Plantago*, comes from the Latin word 'planta', which means 'sole of the foot'.

FEED THE BIRDS

Most people are aware that birds eat berries, but did you also know that they eat plant seeds, too? Songbirds love a plantain-seed snack – just like us!

SOOTHING A SAXON

The Anglo Saxons – who settled in Britain 1,600 years ago – believed plantain possessed special healing powers. They used it for treating wounds, boils, bruises and to reduce pain or swelling. The leaves of the plantain would be wrapped round injuries such as splinters, poisonous snake bites and infections, as it was thought that the plant could draw out the poison and splinters from the skin.

Recently, scientists discovered that the Saxons might have had the right idea about plantain. It can indeed help reduce inflammation and aid the healing of wounds. In fact, we still use plantain for its healing properties today. The leaves are used in the same way we use the dock plant for soothing stings and itchy bites. When squished up and mixed with a bit of water, the leaves have a soothing effect when applied to the skin. If you get stung by a stinging nettle, and are near plantain, pick a leaf, add a little water and rub this on the sting – it should help ease the pain.

THE NINE HERBS CHARM

The Saxons loved plantain. It was a plant that grew in abundance all year long and it helped heal wounds and reduce pain. What's not to love?! They even wrote a poem about the plant, which is part of the 'Nine Herbs Charm'. This long poem contains remedies, prayers, blessings and charms, and is believed to have been written in the 10th or 11th century. It is a beautiful, mysterious piece of writing, handed down through generations, and was a way of sharing knowledge about herbs and plants.

In the charm, the Saxons call plantain waybread. This beautiful section of the poem celebrates the spirit and resilience of waybread . . .

And you, Waybread, mother of plants
open to the east, mighty within,
carts ran over you, ladies rode over you,
brides cried over you, bulls snorted over you,
you withstood them all and you were crushed,
so may you withstand the poison and infection
and the evil that travels round the land.

PINEAPPLE WEED

WHAT DOES IT LOOK LIKE? Pineapple weed grows low to the ground, only ever reaching around 30 cm in height. The plant has round, cone-shaped flower heads that are yellow in colour with a slight tinge of green. These flower heads look just like chamomile flowers, but without the white petals. If you squint while peering at the flowers, they look almost like pineapples. The leaves are narrow and **feathery** with small gaps in between each one.

WHERE DOES IT GROW? Weeds grow almost anywhere, and the pineapple weed is no exception. You'll find it in lots of places, but most often on disturbed ground and farmland pathways.

SCIENTIFIC NAME *Matricaria discoidea*

NICKNAMES Wild chamomile, mayweed, disc mayweed, rayless mayweed

PARTS YOU CAN EAT Leaves and flowers

BEST TIME TO PICK IT Pineapple weed blooms throughout spring and summer.

THE FORAGER'S DICTIONARY
FEATHERY

When a leaf is described as feathery, it means it has many small and delicate pieces, which gives it the appearance and feel of a feather.

WHAT CAN YOU DO WITH IT?

A fruity squishy nibble

When you squish pineapple weed between your fingers, it releases a nice fruity smell, similar to pineapple. You can also experience the pineapple taste if you give the leaves a little nibble. Try it out for yourself!

Relaxing summer drinks

If you enjoy the pineapple weed's fruity flavour, you can make it into a fantastic summer drink, such as iced tea or a refreshing cordial.

I DIDN'T KNOW THAT!

A RECORD BREAKER

Pineapple weed could have originally come to the UK from Asia. Its first sighting over here was in 1871. Within a relatively short time, this plant had covered the entire country, making it officially one of the fastest-spreading plants of the 20th century.

WHERE DOES ITS FRUITINESS COME FROM?

Pineapple weed earned its name because of its smell and taste. This amazing plant's superpower comes from an oil called myrcene, which is found in pineapple weeds and many other plants. Squishing the weed between your fingers releases this oil and the pineapple smell. Myrcene is also used in some perfumes.

FORAGER'S CHALLENGE

1. Find and identify some pineapple weed.

2. Squish the plant between your fingers to experience its fruity smell.

BROAD-LEAVED DOCK

WHAT DOES IT LOOK LIKE?
Broad-leaved docks have oval-shaped leaves, which have a pointed tip (a bit like the tip of a spear). These leaves can grow to a huge size, reaching up to 30 cm in length, and are slightly wavy in shape. The **veins** flow out from a centre spine, covering the leaf in a majestic swirl pattern. They can sometimes have a tinge of red to them, which gives the plant its alternative name: red-veined dock. By early summer, the dock produces tall reddish-brown flower stalks that can grow to around 1 m in height. At this time of year, the plant also produces thousands of seeds.

WHERE DOES IT GROW?
You'll find dock plants growing pretty much anywhere.

SCIENTIFIC NAME
Rumex obtusifolius

NICKNAMES
Bitter dock, red-veined dock, dock leaf, butter dock

PARTS YOU CAN EAT
The leaves, stem and seeds. Though it's important not to eat too much! Oxalic acid is what makes dock taste sour. You shouldn't eat too much of it because it can cause kidney stones and anyone prone to kidney stones should not eat dock. Eat no more than 2 leaves at a time, and only do so now and again.

BEST TIME TO PICK IT
Its leaves are fresh in spring but still fine to eat in the summer. In the summer you'll also be able to get hold of the seeds.

THE FORAGER'S DICTIONARY
VEIN

When you look at any type of leaf, you might notice it has lines on its surface. These are called veins, and they actually work in a similar way to human veins. Plant veins transport water, nutrients and energy all around the plant to keep it healthy and strong.

WHAT CAN YOU DO WITH IT?
Eat it fresh!

Old dock leaves don't taste very nice, but it's easy to find fresh young ones, and these have a surprisingly sweet, lemony taste. Want to know how fresh your dock is? Try breaking off a dock leaf from the base of its stem. You'll be able to tell straight away how fresh it is by how slimy the stem is when it breaks away. The slimier the stem, the fresher the dock leaf!

All in moderation

The dock leaves can also be added to salads or used to wrap up spring rolls. However, broad-leaved dock contains oxalic acid, which can be toxic when consumed in large amounts. This chemical is also found in spinach and even chocolate, so it's nothing to worry about. But the oxalic acid (which makes the leaf taste sour), can also cause kidney stones, so anyone prone to kidney stones should not eat it.

I DIDN'T KNOW THAT!

THOUSANDS OF BIRTHDAYS

A large broad-leaved dock can produce up to 60,000 ripe seeds per year, and these seeds can grow into new broad-leaved docks. These seeds are also capable of surviving in undisturbed soil for over 50 years! Imagine looking after 60,000 children — birthdays would get very confusing indeed.

FRESH, COLD BUTTER

In the olden days, this plant was known as 'butter dock' because people wrapped it around butter in order to keep the butter fresh and cool when selling at the market.

THE DOCKINATOR!

The broad-leaved dock is the Terminator of the plant world. If you chop off its head (the bit above ground), it will simply grow back!

FORAGER'S CHALLENGE

1. Find and identify a broad-leaved dock.

2. Make a dock-leaf balm for soothing stings (see page 77).

SOOTHING SLIME

You're probably aware that the dock plant is traditionally used to soothe a sting from a stinging nettle. As pioneering nurse Mary Seacole said: 'Beside the nettle ever grows the cure for its sting'. And it's true that the two plants can often be found side by side.

But do you know how to actually use a dock leaf to cure a sting? The common method is to take the leaf and rub it on the sting with a bit of saliva. But in fact, the most effective way to use a dock leaf is by squeezing the juice out from the lower stem of the plant. The juice is the thing that cools the sting, so this is a much better technique for soothing that nasty stinging feeling!

For many years scientists were unable to find out why the leaves had a soothing effect. There isn't a special chemical in dock leaves that makes them particularly good at this job. Then they realized that it could be the way the dock-leaf slime evaporates from the skin. This is why it's important to use the dock-leaf juice, and not just rely on the leaf itself.

LOVE IS IN THE AIR

A slightly different type of dock plant (called a curly dock) was once thought to be a powerful love potion. But creating this 'potion' was very complicated! You had to dig up the dock root, dress it to resemble the person you want to love you, then carry this around in your pocket for an entire month. Then you had to chop the root into slices, boil it and use the root water to wash yourself with. It was believed this would make the person your heart desired fall in love with you.

Amazingly, this love potion ended up being used by shop owners in an attempt to gain more customers – a belief thought to have started in medieval Europe. The shop owners, instead of washing in this love potion, would wipe it on their door handles in the hope that customers would fall under its spell and fall in love with the store. Some shop owners even started mopping the entire shop floor with the potion! We'd love to know if this ever worked . . .

BROAD-LEAVED DOCK RECIPE

SOOTHING DOCK AND PLANTAIN BALM

A balm is a fragrant cream or liquid used to heal and soothe the skin. Here's how to make your very own from plantain and broad-leaved dock.

EQUIPMENT

Large, deep saucepan
Large glass bowl
Small oven-proof dish
Clean dishcloth
Small container(s), washed thoroughly and rinsed

INGREDIENTS

5–10 fresh dock leaves, finely chopped
5–10 plantain leaves, finely chopped
1 cup cocoa butter (or soya wax)

It's important not to apply a balm to broken skin. If in doubt, make sure you speak to a doctor!

METHOD

1. Preheat your oven to 50°C /120°F.

2. Fill the saucepan with cold water, then place it on a hob on a medium heat. Place the large glass bowl in the water and add your cocoa butter to the bowl. (Make sure your adult is around to help with this step!)

3. The butter should begin to slowly melt. Ensure you keep stirring as it melts.

4. Add your chopped leaves to the oven-proof dish, then pour the melted butter over the top of them. Make sure the leaves are completely covered in the butter.

5. Put the oven-proof dish in the oven and turn the oven off. Leave for 1 to 3 hours. This is so the butter can soak up all the goodness from the leaves.

6. Remove the dish from the oven and pour the liquid through the cloth to filter out any leftover plant material.

7. Pour the mixture into your container(s) and put in the fridge overnight, so the balm can set. Store in a cool, dry place. Balms can last many years if stored in this way.

BURDOCK

WHAT DOES IT LOOK LIKE?

To identify and forage burdock, you need to understand how old it is. This is because burdock is what's known as a biennial plant, which means it has two stages in its life.

In the first year of its growth, the burdock is fresh and yummy to eat. But in the second year, it goes soft and doesn't taste very nice at all. Luckily it's easy to tell if a burdock plant is young and suitable for foraging.

In their first year, the burdock leaves are *huge* (remember the film *Jurassic Park* – they look a bit like the plants in that!). The leaves grow low to the ground in the shape of a **rosette**. They have a sort of elongated heart shape, with two deep lobes at the bottom, where the leaf joins the stem. When you look at the topside of the leaf, you'll see that, like most leaves, it's bright green. But turn it over, and you might be surprised to see the underside has a soft white colour that feels woolly to the touch – a bit like a jumper.

When you look at the veins on the topside of the leaf you can see that they

THE FORAGER'S DICTIONARY
ROSETTE

When a plant is described as growing in a rosette, it means that as the plant grows out of the ground, the leaves cluster together to form a circular pattern.

split and head off in different directions before reaching the leaf's edge. The edges of the burdock leaf are also slightly wavy all the way round. The stem of the burdock tends to fade in colour, from green to a reddish purple, as it heads towards the ground.

In its second year, the burdock transforms into an even larger plant that can grow to nearly 2 m in height! It also now produces flowers, which have a spherical shape and are purple in colour. In fact, they look similar to thistle flowers. When these flowers dry out (normally in late autumn or winter), they become known as burs. Burs are actually balls that contain burdock seed. They attach to animal fur, and our clothes, and are a way for the burdock to spread its seeds far and wide so new burdock plants can spring up.

WHERE DOES IT GROW?
Once you learn how to recognize burdock, you'll see it everywhere! It can most often be found in grasslands, gardens, woodlands, wetlands and around farmers' fields.

SCIENTIFIC NAME
Arctium lappa or *Arctium minus*

NICKNAMES
Thorny bur, beggar's buttons

PARTS YOU CAN EAT
Leaves, stem and root

BEST TIME TO PICK IT
In the first year of a burdock's life, you can eat the leaves in spring and early summer, when they're fresh. However, the roots are the most popular part of the burdock, and these can be dug up in spring and autumn.

WHAT CAN YOU DO WITH IT?
Eat the roots!
Burdock roots are a tasty vegetable, similar to parsnips or carrots. The root is absolutely jam-packed with goodness. In fact, a single cup of cooked burdock root contains 26.4 g of

carbohydrate, 2.6 g of protein and 2.2 g of fibre. It's also an amazing source of vitamin B6, manganese, potassium, magnesium and phosphorus. We think the best way to eat the root is by baking some burdock-root chips (see page 83 for the recipe!), but you can use them in any way you'd use any other root veggie.

I DIDN'T KNOW THAT!

THE ROOT OF THE PROBLEM

There is a catch when it comes to burdock roots. Sadly, you aren't allowed to dig up the roots of wild burdock! This doesn't mean you can't get hold of them. Some of you might have burdock in your garden, and it can still be bought in shops, where it's sold as a regular vegetable, much like carrot or parsnip. If digging up burdock root from your garden, make sure you get the homeowner's permission, and that you have an adult to help you.

FORAGER'S CHALLENGE

1. Find and identify a burdock plant.

2. Bake some burdock-root chips (see page 83).

For centuries, burdock has been famous around the world for the healing properties that it is believed to possess. Its seeds, roots and leaves have been made into drinks to treat illnesses such as colds, flu, gout, constipation and to break up kidney and bladder stones (if you're not sure what these last two are, **ask an adult** – all we'll say is that they're very painful!).

ONE SMALL STEP FOR MAN, ONE GIANT LEAP FOR BURDOCK

Did you know burdock has actually changed the world? This is a remarkable story, and it starts with a man called George de Mestral who, one day in 1941, went out for a walk with his dog. George strode through the countryside and found himself suddenly covered in the burdock's sticky burs. He began to wonder: 'How on earth do these burs stick to my clothes?'

But this wasn't just a passing thought. In fact, it obsessed George for ages! After many years of hard work, he finally figured out the answer to his question and was able to successfully create a material that acted just like the bur. This took the form of two strips of fabric – one with thousands of tiny hooks and another with thousands of tiny loops. Designed in this way, the fabric could stick together.

Can you guess what he named his invention? Velcro! That's right. That material that tightens your shoes and the back of your cap wouldn't exist if it wasn't for the burdock plant. And Velcro doesn't only tighten shoes, it's used for many important things such as life-saving medical equipment and even spaceships – it holds parts of astronauts' spacesuits together!

BURDOCK RECIPES

DANDELION AND BURDOCK DRINK

This delicious drink takes a bit of effort to make, but they say the greatest views come after the hardest climbs, and dandelion and burdock is well worth the effort!

EQUIPMENT

Large, deep pan with lid
Slotted spoon
Clean dishcloth
Jug

For more about dandelions see page 124.

INGREDIENTS

1 burdock root, washed and peeled
A few dandelion roots
3 cups water
1 thumb-length piece of ginger, peeled and sliced into small chunks
1 cup honey

METHOD

1. Chop your roots into slices – these should be about the thickness of a pound coin.

2. Add them and the ginger to your pan with the water.

3. Pop the lid on to the pan and bring the water to the boil. Once the water is bubbling away, reduce the heat and let it simmer for 30 minutes.

4. Use a slotted spoon to check your roots are cooked through. The best way to do this is to lift them out of the water with the spoon, and (getting an adult to help you) pierce the root with a knife. If it slides in easily, you know your roots are cooked.

5. Once cooked, turn off the heat and remove the roots from the water with the spoon. These can now be thrown away – ideally in a compost bin!

6. When the water is cool, place your dishcloth over a jug and pour the water through it and into the jug. This will filter out any root remnants.

7. Pour the honey into the jug and stir until the juice is infused (you'll know this has happened when all the honey has disappeared).

8. Now you can enjoy your drink – either from a glass or poured into a bottle (washed and rinsed) to carry around with you. We like to mix it with sparkling water, which means it tastes just like cola! If placed in a sealed bottle, your cordial will last a few days in the fridge.

BURDOCK-ROOT CHIPS

This is a great way to turn your burdock roots into crispy chips, which have a delicious, nutty flavour.

EQUIPMENT

Peeler
Baking tray lined with baking paper
Deep saucepan
Wooden spoon

INGREDIENTS

1 burdock root (about the size of a parsnip or a
   large carrot), peeled
salt and pepper

METHOD

1. Preheat your oven to 150°C/300°F

2. Chop your roots into slices – these should be about the thickness of a pound coin. Place these on your baking tray.

3. Bake in your oven until they are soft in the middle and crispy on the outside (this will take 10 to 20 minutes depending on the thickness of your chips). Add some salt and pepper, and enjoy!

4. Once cooked, add salt and pepper, and then enjoy your tasty burdock-root snack!

ROSEBAY WILLOWHERB

WHAT DOES IT LOOK LIKE? Rosebay willowherb can grow to over 2 m in height! Its stems are a red or green colour with a soft **pith** centre. Its leaves are long and spear-shaped, and spiral round the stem. They do this until about three quarters of the way up the plant, where soft tube-shaped seed pods then emerge – these are pink in colour but fade to green underneath the pod. The leaves have a unique vein pattern, which we can use to help identify the plant. Its veins branch out from the centre spine of each leaf, but don't quite reach the edge of it. They instead turn back towards the centre, creating a curving pattern. The flowers have four bright pink petals.

WHERE DOES IT GROW? Rosebay willowherb loves to grow on disturbed open ground. Disturbed ground means the soil has been changed from its natural condition – after a fire, for instance.

SCIENTIFIC NAME *Chamaenerion angustifolium*

NICKNAMES Fireweed, bombweed

PARTS YOU CAN EAT Stem, leaves and flowers

BEST TIME TO PICK IT In early spring the plant is only about 20 cm tall, but you can still eat its young shoots (small leaves and stem). The flowers and fully grown leaves can then be eaten in late summer.

THE FORAGER'S DICTIONARY
PITH
This is a soft, spongy (or sometimes jelly-like) centre found within a stem.

WHAT CAN YOU DO WITH IT?

Bright pink edible flowers!

You can eat the flowers fresh, add them to salads for a splash of colour or infuse them in jams and syrups. Infusing is a way of adding flavour from one substance to another; for example, from plants and flowers in food or drink. If you infuse jams or syrups with rosebay flowers, they turn bright pink!

Secret jelly

In the summer, when rosebay is fully grown and covered with pink flowers, the stem is filled with a cucumber-flavoured pith. If you split the stem in two, you can scoop this jelly out and eat it.

Wild asparagus

The fresh young shoots are wonderfully soft and make a great alternative to asparagus. They are also an excellent accompaniment to a meal – just like asparagus – or you can pickle them (check out how to do this on page 87).

I DIDN'T KNOW THAT!

A FLOWERY TIME MACHINE

Rosebay willowherb is known as fireweed. It's called this because it loves to grow on ground where there has been a fire – even if the fire happened a long time ago. During the Second World War it also became known as bomb weed. This was because rosebay would often grow in places where bombs had fallen and left burnt holes in the earth.

SEEDS, SEEDS, EVERYWHERE

Late in summer, the rosebay's seed pods open and release little fluffy seeds. If you catch rosebay at the right time, you can see thousands of these seeds fill the air, which is an incredible sight. A single rosebay willowherb plant can produce up to 80,000 seeds!

FORAGER'S CHALLENGE

1. Find and identify a rosebay willowherb.
2. In summer, try the jelly pith hidden in its stem.

LONG LIVE ROSEBAY!

The rosebay willowherb has been used for a long time as medicine. It's very popular in Alaska among the Dena'ina (one of many tribes of Indigenous Peoples in this area), who use the leaves to help heal wounds and draw out infection from the skin.

But the leaves can also be used for tea – and this is where things get interesting. Tea made from fresh rosebay leaves was used for a long time to soothe digestive issues such as diarrhoea. Today, this tea is still popular among campers, who use it as a quick fix for an upset tummy!

The leaves can also be used for a special type of tea called Ivan chai. Ivan chai was the favourite tea of a herbalist and doctor named Peter Badmayev, who played a large part in introducing medicine from Tibet to imperial Russia in the late 1800s. He opened a clinic in Russia that only treated its patients with herbs, and it's said that Peter used Ivan chai tea to treat many people, claiming it could extend human life. Now, we aren't saying Peter was definitely right about this, but he did live to the ripe old age of 109! Do you think ivan chai tea was the secret to Peter's long life?

ROSEBAY WILLOWHERB RECIPE

PICKLED PLANTS

Pickling plants is a brilliant way of preserving them, and it also adds lots of delicious flavour. You can pickle pretty much anything you fancy. We're going to show you our method for pickling the young shoots of rosebay willowherb.

EQUIPMENT

Sharp knife

Large saucepan

Jars (as many as you need – washed thoroughly and rinsed)

INGREDIENTS

5–20 fresh rosebay willowherb shoots

½ cup water

1 cup white wine vinegar or apple cider vinegar

1 tsp salt

1 tsp sugar

1 tsp mustard seeds (optional)

METHOD

1. Prepare your shoots. First, peel off all the leaves except for a sprout of young ones at the top of each stem. Your shoots should look similar to asparagus. Next run your finger down the stem to find the toughest part of the lower stem, then chop it off and wash your shoots.

2. Put the vinegar, water, salt, sugar and mustard seeds into the saucepan, then bring to a simmer. Remove from the heat and allow to cool.

3. If sterilizing in the oven, wait for your jars to cool, then pop your shoots into them. If they don't fit, cut them in half.

4. Pour the liquid into the jar, and allow everything to cool before sealing it with the lid.

5. Leave for about a week, when your shoots will be fully pickled. They will then last for up to four weeks in the fridge.

WILD GARLIC

WHAT DOES IT LOOK LIKE? The leaves are long and bright green with a pointed tip and smooth edges. The flowers grow in delicate white clusters and are star-like with six white petals. The garlic **bulb** is white in colour and lives just underneath the ground, with tiny roots that stick out of the bottom of it. When you crush the leaves, stem or the bulb, it releases a strong smell of garlic.

WHERE DOES IT GROW? Damp, shaded woodlands. Sometimes, if you're lucky, you can find an entire wood full of it!

SCIENTIFIC NAME *Allium ursinum*

NICKNAMES Ramsons, bear's leek, wood garlic

PARTS YOU CAN EAT All of it! Leaves, stem, flowers and roots.

BEST TIME TO PICK IT Late winter and early spring.

Lily of the valley, arum and lords-and-ladies (see page 191) are poisonous plants with similar leaves to wild garlic, and they often grow alongside it. When you are picking wild garlic make sure you look carefully at every leaf you are picking. They should all smell garlicky, or you shouldn't eat them!

THE FORAGER'S DICTIONARY
BULB

A bulb is a sort of underground storage chamber for a plant. The plant uses its bulb to store nutrients – substances that feed the plant and help it survive. Much like how we store our food in cupboards, plants store their food in bulbs!

WHAT CAN YOU DO WITH IT?

Make fresh garlic nibbles

Wild garlic makes a fantastic wild nibble and has a yummy flavour, which means it's a favourite of many foragers. The young leaves are delicious, but you can also eat the flowers, which appear later in the year.

Get food for free

Wild garlic can be used in just the same way you might use garlic bought from the shop. The only difference is it's free! The leaves make an excellent garlic pesto and are also great additions to salads and soups.

I DIDN'T KNOW THAT!

BEARS LOVE WILD GARLIC

Did you know that there used to be wild brown bears in Europe? These bears would roam the lands doing what bears do best – scratching their backs and eating wild food. One plant the bears loved in particular was wild garlic, which is why the plant is also known as bear's leek. Imagine a bear roaring at you with garlic breath – yuck!

CHEMICAL REACTION

When garlic is chopped, crushed or chewed, a chemical reaction takes place that releases the powerful, unique smell and taste. You can still smell garlic in its natural form, but the whiff is just not as strong.

GARLIC IS GOOD FOR YOU!

Studies have found that garlic which grows in the wild has higher amounts of vitamins and minerals than the garlic you buy in the supermarket. Wild garlic contains vitamins C and B6, manganese, selenium, phosphorus, thiamine, calcium and iron and it is especially rich in magnesium.

FORAGER'S CHALLENGE

1. Find and identify wild garlic.
2. Try crushing a garlic leaf to release that famous smell!

STRONG AS LEAD

Garlic is consumed in many different cultures around the world. It's even been found in ancient Egyptian pyramids.

But it wasn't just the ancient Egyptians who ate garlic. Greek Olympians and ancient Roman soldiers used garlic to help them become faster and stronger. So when adults say eat your greens, this is why!

Garlic was also thought to help stop and heal infections. In fact, when scientists decided to take a bite out of garlic to see what was in it, they found a long list of strange and wonderful things. Firstly, they discovered that garlic contains chemicals called 'organo sulphur compounds'. These chemicals are only released when garlic is crushed and are what give it that unique smell and taste.

But these garlic-breathed scientists found something else. They realized that the plant was able to help remove a particularly nasty element from our bodies: lead. Lead is a poisonous metal that is bad for us if it gets into our systems. Lead attacks the brain and central nervous system and causes lots of problems, so it's a good thing garlic is on hand to help.

CREATURES OF THE NIGHT

You've probably heard that vampires are scared of garlic, right? But why are these blood-sucking monsters so afraid of a little plant?

No one knows for sure. It could be because garlic was so smelly that it scared the vampires away! In order to protect themselves from vampires, people rubbed garlic rubbed it all over their bodies, with extra garlic for foreheads and armpits, so they could smell as garlicky as possible! Garlic was hung in windows and even rubbed on doors.

Amazingly, garlic does protect people from a real-life blood-sucking enemy – but it isn't vampires. Mosquitoes suck blood when they bite (and your skin then becomes red and itchy – if you've ever been bitten by a mosquito, you'll know what we mean!), and can carry life-threatening diseases in some countries (though not in the UK). They hate garlic, and skin covered in garlic can repel mosquitoes for up to 40 minutes. Perhaps people made a connection between being protected from one blood-sucking creature and decided it also protected them from another!

STINGING NETTLE

WHAT DOES IT LOOK LIKE? Nettles can grow to be massive – nearly 2.5 m tall in the right soil! They're a bright shade of green all over, and their leaves are serrated with a pointed tip. These leaves can grow up to several centimetres long and look like a classic drawing of a heart. If you peer really closely at a nettle leaf and its stem, you'll see they're covered in what appear to be tiny hairs. These hairs, called **trichomes**, are actually hollow, and are what give the nettle its infamous sting.

WHERE DOES IT GROW? You can find stinging nettles pretty much anywhere. But their favourite places to grow are on empty stretches of ground, disturbed soils and hedgerows.

SCIENTIFIC NAME *Urtica dioica*

NICKNAMES Burn hazel, devil's claw

PARTS YOU CAN EAT Leaves and stem (though they must be cooked!). Only young nettle leaves can be eaten, though. Old nettle leaves contain little crystals called cystoliths that can irritate your kidneys. When the nettle plant is flowering, and once its seeds have been formed, the leaves are too old to be eaten.

THE FORAGER'S DICTIONARY
TRICHOMES

These are the stinging nettle's hair-like needles, and they are extremely fragile. If you brush your bare skin against these needles, they break off and pierce your skin, injecting you with a cocktail of chemicals that cause mild pain and itching.

BEST TIME TO PICK IT Nettles grow all year round, but are most common between spring and autumn. **It's important to always wear gloves when picking nettles, so you don't get stung.**

WHAT CAN YOU DO WITH IT?
Not eat it, surely . . .

Sounds ridiculous, right? Who on earth would eat a stinging nettle?! Well, nettles are actually delicious to eat, and once cooked, they lose all of their sting so are completely safe for us to consume. There are many ways you can eat stinging nettles, from nutritious soups, stinging-nettle bread and pasta, to pesto, tea, smoothies and hummus! You can even make stinging-nettle crisps, cake and juice!

I DIDN'T KNOW THAT!

FULL OF GOODNESS

Did you know that the stinting nettle is considered one of the most nutritious plants on Earth? This is because it is full of vitamins and minerals, including vitamins A, C and K, as well as protein, iron, magnesium and several B vitamins. Calcium is great for helping young bones (like yours) grow strong and healthy, and nettles have a whopping four times the amount of calcium than broccoli or spinach!

IT'S EASY BEING GREEN

The nettle's bright green colour means it's a great dye. The colour can be extracted from the plant and used to give colour to fabric. In fact, there's a rumour that nettles were used during the Second World War for the green uniforms worn by British soldiers.

HOME SWEET HOME

You wouldn't think it to look at them, but stinging nettles are actually an ideal home for a very familiar bug: the ladybird. The nettle provides them with food and shelter.

THAT BURNING FEELING

The proper name for the stinging nettle is *Urtica dioica*. This name comes from the Latin word 'uro' which means 'to burn'. If you've ever been stung by a stinging nettle, you can probably guess why they landed on that name!

FORAGER'S CHALLENGE

1. Find and identify some stinging nettles.

2. Be brave – try making a recipe with stinging nettles (these can be found on page 96 onwards).

PAIN RELIEF

We know stinging nettles are really good for us and contain all sorts of stuff our bodies need to be fit and healthy.

It was also once thought that stinging nettles could ease the pain of arthritis, which is a condition affecting the joints in our bodies, making it difficult and painful to move around. It was believed that being stung by nettles could help with the discomfort. This belief has been around for thousands of years, and there is some evidence to suggest that ointments made from nettles do indeed help ease pain from arthritis and inflammation (swelling that arises from injury).

GOD OF NETTLES

You may recognize the name Loki. Today, he's probably more famous than ever thanks to some very well-known films and TV shows! Dressed all in green and fighting against and alongside other gods and superheroes, he's actually been around – in myths and legends in many different forms – for thousands of years.

Believed by the Vikings to be the god of mischief, in ancient Norse mythology Loki was said to have got up to all sorts of naughty things, sometimes helping his fellow gods, but more often than not playing tricks and wreaking havoc.

What you might not know, however, is that Loki had a magical fishing net made of stinging nettles. This net doesn't appear in many films and TV shows, but given that it was very important to Loki we're sure he'd be a bit annoyed that it's been left out! It's believed he used the fishing net for catching salmon.

Here is one of our favourite tales featuring the god of mischief. The story also stars Idun again, Norse goddess of spring and rejuvenation. Idun, you'll remember, was the keeper of magic apples, which the gods had to eat so they could stay young and beautiful.

Loki thought it would be fun to trick a giant called Thiassi into stealing Idun and her apples. Without these apples, time poured into the heavens, giving the gods wrinkles and grey hair – much to their annoyance!

STINGING NETTLE RECIPES

⚠️ **Safety advice**: before stinging nettles are cooked, it's important to **always** wear gloves when handling them. Ideally these should be marigolds, and they should be clean. This is so you don't get stung! With all recipes you should have an adult helping you, but it's especially important that you cook with an adult when it comes to these stinging nettle recipes.

STINGING NETTLE CAKE

Stinging nettles might seem a bit mean, but they can actually be baked into a delicious cake!

EQUIPMENT

Large saucepan
Sieve
Blender
Mixing bowl
Whisk (manual or electric)
Cake tin lined with baking paper

INGREDIENTS

Stinging nettle leaves (enough to fill
    one large bowl)
6 tbsp butter
6 tbsp sugar
4 eggs
½ courgette (optional), grated
8 tbsp self-raising flour

METHOD

1. Preheat the oven to 180°C/350°F.

2. Put your nettle leaves into the saucepan, **ask an adult** to pour over some boiling water and let them blanch for 3–4 minutes. (Blanching simply involves leaving veg or leaves in hot water for a short time; in this case, it will wilt and soften the leaves.)

3. Strain the leaves through the sieve and then pop them into the blender. Whizz to a puree, which is when the mixture is completely smooth.

4. Pour through the sieve again to get rid of any excess water, then put to one side.

5. Put the butter and sugar in the mixing bowl and mix together.

6. Add the eggs and a pinch of flour, and whisk until the mixture is light and fluffy (this will be quicker with an electric whisk – but is still possible with a manual one!).

7. Now add in your nettle puree and gently fold it into the mixture. Add your grated courgette at this point, if using, and stir into the mixture.

8. Make a little hole in the middle of your mixture and add in the flour. Stir it using a gentle figure-of-eight motion. If your cake mix is looking a bit too runny, simply add in a few more tablespoons of flour.

9. Pour the mixture into the cake tin and put in the oven for 30–45 minutes.

10. To tell if your cake is ready, pop a skewer through the middle of it. If it comes out clean (without any crumbs or mixture on it), the cake is ready.

11. Leave to cool in the tin for 10 minutes, then turn the cake out on to a plate. Cut a slice and enjoy!

STINGING NETTLE CRISPS

Did you know that any leafy greens can be transformed into sweet or savoury crisps? Even stinging nettles, which are particularly tasty!

EQUIPMENT

Colander
Mixing bowl
Baking tray lined with baking paper

INGREDIENTS

Stinging-nettle leaves (as much as you want, but we like enough to fill one large bowl)
½ tsp salt (or seasoning of your choice – this could be curry powder, garlic, pepper or paprika)
3 tsp oil

METHOD

1. Preheat the oven to 150°C/300°F.

2. Wearing your gloves, pop all your nettles into a colander and give them a good wash under the tap with cold water.

3. Add the salt (or other seasoning) and oil to your bowl and mix together.

4. Still wearing your gloves, add the leaves to the bowl and cover them in the oil and salt mixture.

5. Still wearing the gloves, place your nettles on the baking tray so you have one layer of them (use another baking tray if you have too many leaves).

6. Put in the oven and bake for about 10 minutes. Check on the leaves regularly – they should be nice and crispy when ready, but you want to avoid burning them!

Flowers! Bright and bold,
with their happy colours and beautiful
scents, flowers make us smile, decorate
gardens and grow wild and free all around us.

But what lots of people don't realize is that flowers can be
eaten, too. Dandelions, daisies, roses, and many more can be
eaten fresh, or made into teas, cordials or syrups. The list of
ways we can enjoy edible flowers is endless. They can even
make our homemade foods change colour, and infuse them
with a wonderful scent.

There's a lot of foraging fun to be had with
flowers, and in the following pages you might
even learn about their mythical
healing properties . . .

FLOWERS

HERB ROBERT

WHAT DOES IT LOOK LIKE? Herb robert grows low to the ground, getting up to around 50 cm in height. Its flowers are small, bright pink and star-shaped, normally with five petals. Its leaves are **palmate** and dark green, though they turn red the more they're exposed to sunlight. The stems are often a reddish colour with noticeable hairs protruding from the surface.

WHERE DOES IT GROW? You'll find herb robert growing in shady places, such as woodland, or around the bases of trees, rocks and walls.

SCIENTIFIC NAME *Geranium robertianum*

NICKNAMES Red robin, stinky bob, fox geranium

PARTS YOU CAN EAT Leaves, stem and flowers

BEST TIME TO PICK IT It's best to pick herb robert when it's flowering, which is during the spring and summer.

THE FORAGER'S DICTIONARY
PALMATE

When a leaf is described as palmate, it means the leaf's lobes (the round or pointed parts that stick out from it) spread out from the same point. They do this in much the same way our fingers spread out from the palm of our hand. These leaves are 'palm-like' – hence the name!

WHAT CAN YOU DO WITH IT?

Squish and sniff!

When its leaves are crushed, herb robert releases a
strong smell, which is remarkably similar to the
smell of burning tyres. This is why the plant is also
known as stinky bob!

The Marmite leaf

The smell of herb robert is certainly odd. Some people
love it, others hate it. If you quite like the smell, you
might want to make yourself a nice cup of herb robert
tea or add the leaves and flowers to salads and soups.
If you don't enjoy the smell, that's OK! Perhaps you can
make a tea for someone who does.

I DIDN'T KNOW THAT!

SKIN DEEP

Herb robert is a favourite of many creatures – bees, hoverflies,
moths and others love its distinctive smell. However, mosquitoes are not
a fan! Much like garlic, if you squish a bit of herb robert on to your skin, it
might well stop those pesky critters from giving you a nibble.

A HERB BY ANY OTHER NAME . . .

Although we've given you a few of herb robert's nicknames, it's
estimated that this plant has loads.
Here are just a handful that we think are pretty cool:

- **Death-come-quickly** – no, herb robert isn't poisonous, but it
  was once believed that finding the plant in your house meant
  you'd been cursed by a mischievous goblin known as Puck.

- **Bloodwort** – because the plant turns from green to red in the sun, it
  was believed to be good for our blood!

- **Felonwort** – the condition 'felon finger' arises from a bacterial infection in the end of
  your finger. This can be caused by a cut or scrape, and can be quite painful. Herb robert
  was once thought to heal this infection.

FORAGER'S CHALLENGE

1. Find and identify herb robert.

2. Squish the leaves and smell their unique scent.

BLOOD, GLORIOUS BLOOD

Herb robert was once thought to heal all sorts of illnesses and injuries. Because of its distinctive red colour, people in medieval Europe used to believe it was good for their blood. The leaves would be picked and applied to the skin to help heal cuts and skin infections. Some people even popped the leaves up their noses to stop nosebleeds!

Herb-robert tea was also thought to treat everything from stomach upsets and headaches to liver issues. Extract of herb robert can be found in treatments for 'swimmer's ear' (essentially a sore ear) – though only when combined with other plants.

ROBERT WHO?

You might think that Robert is a bit of a strange name for a plant. So why is it called this? Who was Robert?

Well, there are two possible reasons for the name. The first one links back to a famous monk named Saint Robert who lived in the 11th century. It's believed that Robert loved this plant and used it as a cure for infections and illnesses. It's possible that his enthusiasm for herb robert gave it its distinctive name.

Another possibility is someone we've already mentioned – that cheeky goblin known as Puck. In medieval mythology, Puck's other name was Robin Goodfellow, and he's known in old tales and folklore as a naughty fairy (or sometimes a demon or jester). Puck was famous for his pranks and practical jokes. If something mysterious happened in people's homes, such as someone's shoes being left out in the rain, they'd have likely blamed Puck.

But Puck wasn't just a cheeky prankster; he could also be surprisingly nice. It was said that he'd help families with their chores – a little needlework or perhaps some butter-churning. Puck's good deeds could become bad ones if you displeased him, though, and particularly if you didn't pay him for his work. Puck expected an offering of food and milk, which should be left out for him at night. If he felt neglected, that's when he'd steal and play pranks! This folklore goblin inspired the character Puck in William Shakespeare's play, *A Midsummer Night's Dream*.

So, how does Puck link to herb robert? After all, the names don't sound very similar, do they? Some say it's because Puck originates from a goblin of German folklore known as Knecht Ruprecht, which could also mean servant of Rupert – or Robert!

DOG ROSE

WHAT DOES IT LOOK LIKE? Dog rose can grow up to 3 to 4 m tall and forms large unwieldy bushes with thorny stems that reach out in different directions – like spiky tentacles! Its leaves are an **oval shape** with toothed edges, and they are normally dark green on top with a lighter shade of green underneath. The flowers of the dog rose look more like flat, regular flowers than the garden roses you might be familiar with. They are a bright shade of white or pink and have five petals. The fruits of a rose are generally called rosehips, and the dog-rose rosehips are a vibrant shade of red. When you tear these fruits open they have hairy seeds inside.

WHERE DOES IT GROW? People love dog-rose bushes, so you'll often find them growing in gardens. They also thrive in woodlands, scrublands, pathways, beside rivers and in hedgerows.

SCIENTIFIC NAME *Rosa canina*

NICKNAMES Dog berry, witches' briar

PARTS YOU CAN EAT Flowers and rosehips

BEST TIME TO PICK IT Dog rose tends to flower around spring and summer. The rosehips are ready to pick in autumn and winter, and are best to eat after a frost.

THE FORAGER'S DICTIONARY

OVAL SHAPE

When a leaf is described as having an oval shape, this means the widest part of the leaf is in the middle, and the whole thing looks like a sort of stretched circle shape.

WHAT CAN YOU DO WITH IT?

Rose sugar

If you let the rose flowers dry out (to do this, just lay them on a tea towel for a couple of days), then crunch them up with sugar, this creates a colourful sugary mixture that smells just like roses! This can be sprinkled on biscuits or cakes.

Fresh squish!

After a particularly cold night, when the outside world has gone all frosty, the rosehips are filled with a sweet, red, squishy substance. If you squeeze the rosehip, this substance oozes out and can be eaten. It tastes delicious, but DO NOT eat the seeds that emerge after the squish, because they are surrounded by itchy hairs.

Skin remedies

Rosehips are used in some of the most expensive cosmetic products in the beauty industry. Cosmetics are created from natural or human-made substances, and are used on the body, particularly the skin, to improve a person's appearance. Many people believe that rosehips can slow the signs of ageing – although there's no need for you to worry about that, of course!

FORAGER'S CHALLENGE

1. Find and identify some rosehips.

2. Try the fresh rosehip squish straight after the first frosts (or create your own fake frost! – see page 111).

I DIDN'T KNOW THAT!

BETTER THAN ORANGES

Vitamin C is very important for our health, and
for our skin and immune system in particular.
By weight, the little rosehip fruits contain
more vitamin C than oranges!

ROSEHIPS SAVED US!

During the Second World War, rosehips saved our bacon.
Britain was struggling to get hold of fresh fruit that was rich in vitamin C,
so a collective effort was made to forage hundreds of tonnes of rosehips to fulfil the
nation's vitamin needs. These were then turned into rosehip syrup, which was delivered
to the general public along with other rations during the war. We show you how to make
your very own rosehip syrup on page 111!

FAKE FROST

Rosehips start their life hard and soften as the weather gets colder. You can actually trick
rosehips into becoming softer sooner by faking a frost. You do this by putting rosehips
you've collected into the freezer and leaving them overnight. When the rosehips warm up
and thaw out, they become squishy and sweet.

DOG DAYS

Why does this particular rose include the word dog? Seems pretty odd, right? Well, people
used to believe that the roots of this plant contained medicine that could help stop an
infection if you'd been bitten by a wild dog. Wild dogs used to be much more common
than they are now, and their bites were much more likely to give you a nasty illness. A bite
victim could dig up the dog-rose root, boil it to make a cup of dog-rose tea and drink it
(and hope that it would save them from infection!).

ITCHY AND SCRATCHY

The seeds in rosehips are notoriously itchy. This is because they are covered in hairs that
can scratch and irritate. It's important to remove the seeds of rosehip after they are
cooked, for this very reason (we show you how to do this on page 111). They aren't
poisonous but might result in an itchy bum when they exit the body!

ALL AT SEA

The ancient Greeks, Egyptians, Romans and even the Vikings all used dog rose and rosehips for food and medicine. It was believed parts of the plant could impart strength and good health, and reduce pain from swollen joints, headaches and arthritis.

The Vikings in particular loved rosehips. They spent a lot of time at sea and needed that all-important vitamin C to keep themselves going. They'd eat dried rosehips and drink rosehip tea to help them stay healthy. The Egyptians used rosehips to try to stay young and beautiful, and they made the fruits into an oil, which they'd place on their skin.

Remember we told you earlier how rosehip seeds can make you uncomfortable? Well, years ago people used to eat them . . . on purpose. Nasty little creatures called intestinal worms can get into our insides and cause all sorts of problems, and the belief was that the hairs on the seeds would catch the worms and remove them from people's insides on their way out! (Absolutely **do not** try this at home under any circumstances. If you have any sorts of problems with your insides, see a doctor!)

LOVE AND DEVOTION

As seen from ancient Greek myths to TikTok videos, the rose is often associated with love. The two things are inseparable!

But to understand why this is, we need to travel back over 2,500 years, to the time of the ancient Greeks. The Greeks adored roses. They wrote poetry and stories about them.

One ancient Greek story tells that a drop of blood from Uranus, god of the sky, fell into the ocean, where it mixed with the foam of the sea. Over time, a shape began to take form, which eventually became Aphrodite, the Greek goddess of love. (In one version we found, the story goes that as Aphrodite stepped out of the water on to the earth, the sea foam that fell to the ground from her body transformed into white roses).

Later, Aphrodite fell deeply in love with a mortal man named Adonis. But Ares, the Greek god of courage and war, was furious about this and sent a wild boar to kill Adonis while he was out hunting. As Aphrodite hurried to her lover's aid, she scratched herself upon a rosebush, splashing specks of blood onto their soft white petals as she passed. The story goes that this blood turned the roses a deep shade of red. This is how red roses came to symbolize love and devotion and it's why we might give roses as gifts to those we care about – just as Aphrodite cared for Adonis!

DOG ROSE RECIPE

WORLD-WAR-TWO ROSEHIP SYRUP

Please note that this recipe requires the rosehips to be frozen overnight to improve their sweetness.

EQUIPMENT

Large saucepan
Clean, dry dishcloth
Jug
3 medium-sized jars, washed thoroughly and rinsed

INGREDIENTS

3 cups rosehips, rinsed and frozen overnight
1 lemon, chopped into slices
2 cups water
3 cups sugar

METHOD

1. Remove your rosehips from the freezer and defrost them by running under warm water.

2. Chop the top and bottom off your rosehips, and pop them into the saucepan. Give them a little squish – this will help release the juices during cooking.

3. Add the lemon and water into the saucepan and bring the mixture to the boil. Once boiling, turn down the heat and simmer for 20 minutes.

4. Place the dishcloth over the top of the jug, then **ask an adult** to help you pour your mixture through it. This will filter out the lemon, rosehips and rosehip hairs. **It's very important you remove all the hairs!**

5. Pour the mixture back into the saucepan, add the sugar and stir. Bring back to the boil, then simmer uncovered for 45 minute, stirring every 5 minutes.

6. Your syrup is ready when you drop a little on to a cold plate and, as it cools, it goes thick and sticky. If it's not quite there, simmer for another 6 minutes and try again. Once it's ready, put in jars and cool. If the jars are sterilized, they can be stored in a cool, dry place. If not, make sure you put them in the fridge. Your syrup can last for up to a year in or out of the fridge.

ELDER TREE

WHAT DOES IT LOOK LIKE? The elder tree is really easy to identify, even when it loses its leaves in winter. This is because of its unique bark, which is a light creamy-brown colour and super soft to the touch. If you press the bark hard with your hand, you'll see it is squishy, a bit like a cork from a bottle. The flowers of the elder tree (called elderflowers) grow in **umbels** on little green stems and are a creamy-white colour with five petals per flower. Each flower then develops into large clusters of berries (known as elderberries), which are a deep shade of purply-black. Its leaves are green, oval-shaped and toothed, and grow in sets of five.

WHERE DOES IT GROW? Elder trees are pretty common. You'll likely find them in woodlands, along hedgerows, and in fields, towns and gardens.

SCIENTIFIC NAME *Sambucus nigra*

NICKNAMES Elderflower tree, elderberry tree

THE FORAGER'S DICTIONARY
UMBELS

When we talk about umbels in reference to flowers, we mean a group of flowers that grow closely together in the shape of an umbrella. You know the thing some people hold to keep out of the rain? A shape just like that!

HOW LONG DOES IT LIVE FOR?

Elder trees only live for around 60 years – not that long for a tree!

PARTS YOU CAN EAT

You can eat the flowers fresh off the tree, or cooked. If eaten fresh, they taste very pleasant and have a sort of frothy texture to them. The berries have to be cooked or fermented before you eat them. You can't eat the green stalks or leaves – **even if they're cooked**.

BEST TIME TO PICK IT

The elder tree flowers from late spring to early summer. These flowers then transform into elderberries in late summer and autumn.

WHAT CAN YOU DO WITH IT?

Tea time!

When stirred into warm water, elderflowers make a beautiful tea, which has a wonderful floral (flower-like) flavour.

How cordial

Elderflower cordial is a well-known drink and is enjoyed all around the world. You can buy it in shops, pubs and restaurants. But did you know that you can also make this drink yourself?! We think this homemade version is much nicer, and you can find the recipe on page 116.

Coughs and sneezes

Elderberries are a common ingredient in many cold and flu medicines. But this isn't a new thing – people have been using these berries to keep coughs and sneezes at bay for thousands of years.

You'll notice we've only included lifespans for trees. This is because they live much longer lives than plants and flowers. which we find interesting! Plants, on the other hand, are either perennial, biannual or annul, meaning they come back every year or have different growth cycles.

I DIDN'T KNOW THAT!

PRIDE COMES BEFORE A FALL

Elder trees don't live for very long compared to other trees. They live fast and grow fast, and this makes them super fragile. You can easily break an elder-tree branch just by leaning on it, so it's really important that you don't climb on them, or you could fall and hurt yourself – as well as the poor elder tree!

SMELL YOU LATER

You might hear people complaining that the elder tree smells like cat wee . . . but others might disagree! The truth is, if you pick elderflowers on a hot day in late spring or summer, they smell and taste lovely. But if you pick them in autumn – when they're older – they can smell a bit like cat wee and don't taste very nice. If you don't fancy tasting an elderflower to see if it's good to eat, you can tell its age by giving it a light tap. If you see lots of pollen puff into the air, then it's good to go. If not, probably best to give it a miss.

THE MEDICINE CHEST

The elder tree is sometimes known as the medicine chest. As you can probably guess from that nickname, it's been used as medicine throughout the ages. Mostly it was thought to solve problems with breathing, including bronchitis (an infection in the lungs), coughs, allergies, colds, flu and sore throats. Elderberries were also thought to help reduce the chance of getting sick.

FORAGER'S CHALLENGE

1. Find and identify an elder tree.

2. Make a bottle of the world-famous elderflower cordial (see page 116).

SAY PLEASE

In many cultures, people believed that nature was alive with spirits, gods and all sorts of mystical beings. Many of these beings were thought to live within trees. For the elder tree, it was believed that a being guarded the tree, and this is a myth that's been told all over the world, wherever the tree grows.

In the myths and folktales of Northern Europe, it was believed that the Elder Mother was the guardian. She would haunt or torment people who wanted to build from the wood of the elder tree, unless they asked permission to do so first. In England, the Elder Mother was known as the 'Old girl'. To ask her permission, you had to say out loud to the tree: 'Old woman, give me some of thy wood and I will give thee some of mine when I grow into a tree.'

FIRE IN THE HOLE

The name of the elder tree comes from the Anglo-Saxon word *aeld*. This actually means 'fire' – but why did the Saxons call the elder tree the 'fire tree'? There are two theories. The first is that because the branches of the elder tree are hollow, they may have been used as bellows – a device that blows air into the centre of a fire and helps keep it alight.

The second is a little spookier. People once believed that if you burned the wood of the elder tree the devil would suddenly appear before you!

On a brighter note, the Anglo-Saxons also believed that if you fell asleep under an elder tree when its flowers were in full bloom, you would be invited into the world of the fairies, who would welcome and protect you from evil spirits as you travelled through their realm.

Whatever the reason, the history of the elder tree is certainly full of myths and magic!

ELDERFLOWER RECIPE

ELDERFLOWER CORDIAL

Elderflower cordial is a wonderful drink, which will bring joy to any summer's day!

EQUIPMENT

Large, deep saucepan
Sieve
Jug
Glass bottle, washed thoroughly and rinsed

INGREDIENTS

1 bowl elderflowers, stalks removed (around 30 umbels); once you've collected your elderflowers, take them home **but do not wash them**. You want to keep as much pollen on the elderflowers as possible. The bowl should be about the size of a cereal bowl.
4 cups water
1 lemon or orange, cut into slices
½ cup sugar

METHOD

1. Add the elderflowers to the saucepan.

2. Add the water, orange or lemon, and sugar to the pan and mix everything together.

3. Heat the mixture and bring it to the boil, then lower the heat and simmer for 30 minutes.

4. Strain the liquid through a sieve and into a jug. Use the back of a spoon to squish the elderflowers into the sieve, to ensure you get all that lovely flavour into your cordial.

5. Leave to cool, then pour into a glass bottle and enjoy! This should be stored in the fridge, and will last for a couple of days.

FANCY MAKING SOME NATURAL ICE LOLLIES?

We love ice lollies. They're tasty, refreshing and perfect on a hot day. The ones you can buy in the shop are filled with all sorts of strange ingredients though, which can have you bouncing off the walls!

We think natural ice lollies are much better. They're tastier, fresher and full of lovely goodness.

To make a natural ice lolly, you just need some ice-lolly moulds, homemade cordial and a few fresh flowers (make sure you rinse these first).

To make an elderflower lolly, for instance, pop your elderflowers (washed, of course) in a jug, fill this to the top with warm water and stir (this encourages the flowers to release their fragrance and flavour). To give your ice lollies a touch of sweetness, add in half a teaspoon of honey and stir again. At this stage we then like to add a bit of citrus, such as half a lemon, squeezed, or half an orange, squeezed. This is the fun part, as adding the citrus could change the colour of your mixture! We encourage you to experiment with your mixture – your ice lollies don't have to taste or look perfect the first time.

Pour the mixture into your mould and leave in the freezer until frozen solid. Then remove from the freezer and enjoy!

You could also make ice lollies using your homemade cordial! Fill a jug a quarter of the way with your cordial, fill it up with cold water and then pour into your moulds and freeze.

DAISY

WHAT DOES IT LOOK LIKE?
Daisies can grow up to about 10 cm tall. They are a small flower with white or pinkish petals. These petals grow round its centre (called a **floral disc**), which looks like a bright yellow ball. The daisy's leaves are small and dark green, and they grow in a rosette (a sort of circle) round the bottom of the flowers, in the shape of tiny teaspoons.

WHERE DOES IT GROW?
You can find daisies growing pretty much everywhere!

SCIENTIFIC NAME
Bellis perennis

NICKNAMES
Bruisewort, lawn daisy, bone flower

PARTS YOU CAN EAT
Leaves, stem and flowers

BEST TIME TO PICK IT
You can find daisies all year round, but they are more common in spring and summer.

WHAT CAN YOU DO WITH IT?
Eat it (if you like the flavour!)
Not many people know that daisies can be eaten. They actually taste rather nice, contain lots of stuff that's good for us (including vitamin C) and have a fresh, lemony flavour. Just be sure to wash them first. Some people really like the flower's flavour but others can find the daisy a bit bitter. The only way to find out if you like it is to try one!

THE FORAGER'S DICTIONARY
FLORAL DISC
The centre of a daisy is called the flower head or floral disc. Though it looks like one whole thing, the floral disc is actually made up of tiny individual flowers, which are called disc florets.

Works of art

Daisies are very pretty flowers. If you add a few to a salad, it can make it look like a proper work of art. Or they can be crystallized in sugar and used to decorate cakes.

A healing flower

The daisy is also known as bruisewort or bone flower. This is because daisies contains the natural ability to help our bodies heal from bumps and bruises. (We'll show you how you can use daisies in this way on page 122.)

I DIDN'T KNOW THAT!

DAISY THE CONQUEROR

Daisies are originally from Europe, but they now grow on every single continent on Earth (except for Antarctica). So you could say the daisy has pretty much conquered the entire world!

SECRET NAMES

The daisy wasn't always called a daisy. In Old English (the language spoken in England in the early Middle Ages) it was known as the 'day's eye'. Many people think this name came from the fact that the flower opens up to greet the morning sun, then closes again at night. Its Latin name, *Bellis perennis*, means 'beautiful forever' – two very special names for a very special flower.

FORAGER'S CHALLENGE

1. Find and identify a daisy flower.

2. Try making some daisy bump salve or a lotion bar!

BATTLE SCARS

The daisy is famous for being able to heal bumps and bruises. It is said that the Romans used to soak dressings (bits of material used to put round wounds to help them heal) in daisy-infused water, which they thought would help the wounds heal faster – particularly after a big battle.

Nowadays, you can buy something called arnica gel, which is used to help heal cuts and bruises. This gel is made from the arnica flower, which is a type of daisy that grows in the Alps. We reckon regular daisies are just as good as arnica, and they grow everywhere, not just high up in the mountains.

Tea made from daisies was also used for soothing headaches, and it was believed that chewing a daisy could help with toothache. It's true that daisies do have antimicrobial properties. This means they can help fight bacterial infections, which allows wounds to heal safely and means there's less chance of a scar forming.

THE DAISY AND THE ROSE QUEEN

Have you ever noticed that some daisy petals have a pinkish flush of colour to them? It's almost as if the daisy flower is blushing! There is an old folktale that tells the story of why the daisy has this flush of pink.

Once upon a time, the rose was the queen of the flowers. She announced she was having a birthday party and all the flowers were invited. The little daisy flower never received an invitation to the rose's ball, but she didn't mind – she was too shy to go to a ball anyway and was far happier whispering her congratulations from afar.

But the wind carried the daisy's humble congratulations across the land, all the way to the rose queen. When she heard it, she told the daisy it had nothing to be shy about. 'Your dress is spotlessly white and you have a heart of gold,' she said to the little flower. This compliment made the daisy blush, and it's said that ever since this day the daisy petals have carried a blushing shade of pink.

So the next time you see a blushing daisy, you now know a wonderful story explaining how it came to be, which you can share with friends and family!

DAISY RECIPE

DAISY BUMP SALVE

You now know that arnica gel is used to heal bumps and bruises. Here we are going to show you how to make a salve — a gel-like substance — but made from daisies!

EQUIPMENT

Large, deep saucepan

Heatproof bowl (large enough that the bowl sits at the top of the saucepan and its bottom doesn't touch the water)

Colander

Jug

Small tins or jars , washed thoroughly and rinsed

Be sure NOT to use salve on broken skin, and always make sure you talk to an adult if you're hurt, as something more serious may need medical attention.

INGREDIENTS

1 small bowl fresh or dried daisies (the bowl should be about the size of a cereal bowl)

1 cup solid coconut oil

6 to 8 sprigs lavender or 5 drops lavender oil (optional)

METHOD

1. Ask an adult to fill the saucepan a quarter-full with water and put it on the stove over a medium heat. Rest the heatproof bowl on top of the pan.

2. Bring the water to a light simmer.

3. Add the coconut oil to your bowl and let it melt.

4. Squash your daisies in your hands to release some of the juices, then submerge them in the melted coconut oil using a spoon. If using, add the lavender sprigs or lavender oil.

5. Leave the mixture over a medium heat for a minimum of 1 hour, and a maximum of 1 day (make sure your adult is on hand to help with this). The longer you leave it, the more you'll extract from your daisies (and lavender).

6. Strain the mixture through a colander and into a jug. Use the back of the spoon to squish the daisies against the colander, so you get every last drop of daisy juice!

7. Pour your salve into the tins or jars and put these in the fridge to set.

8. Once set, store in a cool, dry place. Salves can last many years if stored in this way.

DANDELION

WHAT DOES IT LOOK LIKE? The dandelion is probably one of the most recognizable flowers in the world. Its flower head is a bright shade of orange, and the leaves are long and serrated (which means they look spiky). Its stem is green with a purple tinge, and the inside is hollow. The plant's leaves, stem and root leak a white sap when you break or cut into them. The flower of the dandelion ultimately transforms into a fluffy **seed ball** as it ages.

WHERE DOES IT GROW? Dandelions aren't picky. You'll find them growing pretty much anywhere!

SCIENTIFIC NAME *Taraxacum officinale*

NICKNAMES Dent de lion, shepherd's clock, wet-the-bed

PARTS YOU CAN EAT Flowers, leaves and stem

BEST TIME TO PICK IT You can find dandelions all year round, but they are most abundant in spring, summer and autumn.

THE FORAGER'S DICTIONARY
SEED BALL

The dandelion's flower develops into a seed ball as it gets older. The outside of these little seeds are grey in appearance, and the centre a dark brown. Each seed is attached to the centre by a long fuzzy structure called a pappus. This breaks away from the central ball when it's windy, or if someone blows on the ball. This allows the seeds to be carried off to land elsewhere, where it will grow into a brand-new dandelion. In this way, a dandelion can spread itself far and wide!

WHAT CAN YOU DO WITH IT?
Dandelion syrup

Dandelions eaten fresh don't taste so great. But when transformed into syrup, they become a delicious, sticky-sweet treat, which is similar to honey. Dandelions can also be turned into cookies, and we show you how to do this on page 129.

I DIDN'T KNOW THAT!

A LION'S TOOTH

The name dandelion comes from the French *dent-de-lion*, which translates to 'lion's tooth'. This name comes from the fact that if you turn the dandelion leaf sideways, it looks a little bit like the spiky teeth of a lion. Try it for yourself!

A MISUNDERSTOOD FLOWER

Dandelions have a bit of a bad reputation these days. A lot of people think they are bad for their gardens and want to get rid of them. But dandelions are important flowers – they actually heal the earth by drawing up important nutrients from deep in the ground to renew old soil. They also feed insects such as bees and butterflies.

FORAGER'S CHALLENGE

1. Find and identify a dandelion.

2. Try making some dandelion-and-daisy cookies! You can find out how on page 129.

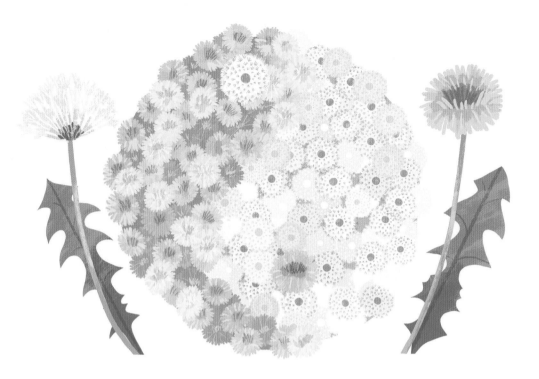

YIN AND YANG

From Europe to China, the dandelion has long been used for healing our bodies. People throughout history have adored dandelions and would be surprised to see how little we care for them today. In traditional Chinese medicine, they call some species of dandelion *pu gong ying* and believe they can release all sorts of harmful stuff from our body to restore its balance.

Ever heard of yin and yang? This phrase is all about balance and helps us understand opposite-but-connected forces. It applies to health as well. In traditional Chinese medicine, it is thought that when our body holds too much heat, the balance between the yin and yang is wrong. In nature, yang is hot and yin is cold, so the dandelion is believed to help restore a harmonious balance between the yin and yang in our bodies.

The dandelion is rich in vitamin K, which allows wounds to heal by helping blood clot. Scientists also reckon that dandelions are good for our liver and digestive system and that they can even help us if we're having trouble going for a wee!

WISH UPON A CLOCK

One of the most widespread beliefs about dandelions is that they can grant us wishes. In order to make a wish, simply find a dandelion that's turned into a seed ball, take a deep breath and blow the seeds away, while making a wish in your mind.

Another belief was that if you got dandelion sap on your skin during the day, you would wet the bed that night. Don't worry, this isn't true! But there is some truth in the claim that dandelions help us to wee – so that's probably where this particular story came from.

Shepherds used to think that dandelions could predict the weather. It was said that if rain was coming, the dandelion would close shut and stay that way until the rains passed. In good weather, the flower heads would open early in the morning and close shut in the evening. So not only can the dandelion predict the weather, but it's a clock as well! This is how it got one of its nicknames: shepherd's clock.

DANDELION RECIPES

DANDELION SYRUP

Dandelion syrup (also known as dandelion honey) is really simple to make and has a beautiful, rich and surprising flavour.

EQUIPMENT

Large, deep saucepan with lid
Sieve
Jug
3 medium-sized jars, washed thoroughly and rinsed

INGREDIENTS

1 big bowl dandelion heads (around 40 to 50)
2 lemons, chopped into slices
1 litre water
1 kg brown sugar

METHOD

1. Give your dandelions a rinse under cold water.

2. Put your dandelions, lemons and water into the saucepan. Put the lid on and bring to the boil.

3. Reduce the heat, take the lid off the pan and leave to simmer for 30 minutes.

4. Pour the mixture through your sieve and into the jug. The dandelions should be left in the sieve.

5. Pour the mixture back into the saucepan and add the sugar. Simmer for 1 hour without the lid on. Scoop off any foam that forms of top of the water – you want your syrup to be clear.

6. After an hour, most of the water should have evaporated from the mixture.

7. Pour the mixture into your jars (wait for them to cool if sterilizing in the oven). As it cools, it will thicken into a gooey, honey-like texture. Yum! (This can last up to a year in or out of the fridge.)

DANDELION-AND-DAISY COOKIES

Impress your friends and family with some incredible dandelion-and-daisy cookies. The flowers give these cookies a delicious taste and texture!

EQUIPMENT

Mixing bowl
Sieve
Rolling pin
Baking tray lined with baking paper
Biscuit cutter (or an empty jar)

INGREDIENTS

½ cup daisy petals and ½ cup dandelion petals (mixed)
1 cup plant-based margarine or butter
½ cup sugar (or ½ cup dandelion syrup – your own if you've made it!)
1 cup plain flour

METHOD

1. Preheat your oven to 180°C (350°F).

2. Put your flower petals into a mixing bowl and add the butter or margarine and the sugar. Use a spoon to mix everything together.

3. Add half the flour into the mixture through a sieve (adding the flour slowly helps create a well-mixed dough).

4. Once the flour is fully combined in the mixture, add the remaining half, mix everything together again and bring it together to form a ball.

5. On a lightly floured surface, roll out your ball of dough so it is about the thickness of a pound coin. Use a biscuit cutter to cut out as many biscuits as you can (the top of a jar also works really well for this). Make sure any petals are smoothed down (as they can burn and not taste very nice). Then put them on the baking tray and in the oven for 20–25 minutes (or until golden brown).

6. Take out of the oven when cooked through and lightly browned, and enjoy.

BORAGE

WHAT DOES IT LOOK LIKE?
It's best to wait until borage is in flower to find it. Otherwise, you may mistake it for something else, as it's not hugely recognizable without its flowers. But you'll know the flowers when you see them, as they look like bright blue stars (though if you're lucky, sometimes you can find them in pink). If you look closely, you can also see they have prominent black **anthers** poking out, which look a little like a bee's antennae. The plant grows to nearly a metre tall, and its stem and leaves are hairy, with the green leaves growing in an oval shape.

WHERE DOES IT GROW?
You can find borage growing in towns, gardens, and along pathways and grasslands.

SCIENTIFIC NAME
Borago officinalis

NICKNAMES
Starflower, bee bread, herb of gladness

PARTS YOU CAN EAT
The flowers

BEST TIME TO PICK IT
The flowers are best in spring and summer.

WHAT CAN YOU DO WITH IT?
Eat the flowers (the best bit!)
Many people would agree that the flowers are the greatest part of the borage plant. Not only do they look like amazing bright blue stars, but they actually taste nice, too. You can snack on these flowers fresh or add them to salads or cakes for decoration.

THE FORAGER'S DICTIONARY
ANTHER
The anther is a part of the stamen, which often appears in the form of stalks at the centre of the flower. This is where the flower's pollen is made. Pollen is a fine, powdery substance produced by flowering plants, which attracts pollinators such as bees and other insects. These insects then carry the pollen to other plants, which allows them to reproduce, creating more of the same plant.

I DIDN'T KNOW THAT!

COLOURING IN

The flowers of the borage are so blue that they can actually be used as food colouring. You can use them to make blue tea or bright blue vinegar. You can even change the colour of the borage flowers themselves. Try this yourself at home. Add some borage flowers to warm water, then add a few drops of lemon juice and watch the colour of the flowers magically transform from blue into bright pink!

PLANT FRIENDS

The borage plant actually protects other flowers and looks after them – a bit like an older sibling. This is known as companion planting. If you put plants that like each other together, you can create a community of plants that provide each other with nutrients and protection from nasty weather, pesky pests and plant diseases. Borage is often planted next to strawberries because it loves to live with the strawberry plant and takes good care of it.

BEE BREAD

Borage is also called 'bee bread'. This is because – like us humans when it comes to bread – bees can't get enough of borage flowers. They love them! Borage flowers produce loads of pollen – so much of it, that if you flick the flowers, you can see the pollen powder puff out into the air. You can even lick it off your hand and see what it's like to be a bee!

FORAGER'S CHALLENGE

1. Find and identify a borage plant in flower.

2. Wait around a borage plant to see if a bee will visit, then watch it buzzing around, collecting borage pollen.

BRAVE BORAGE

Borage is most famous for being used to give people courage. It's said that both the Romans and the Celts (the ancient peoples who lived in Ireland, Scotland and a few other countries over 2,000 years ago) used to mix borage with wine and drink it before great battles, in the belief that it would make them strong and brave.

Others would drink borage to help them feel happy, and in many different countries it's been celebrated for similar reasons. Welsh people used to call borage the herb of gladness. Here is what a few famous people throughout history had to say about the borage plant:

Greek physician Dioscorides

John Evelyn, an English writer and herbalist from the 1600s

Roman historian Pliny the Elder

* someone who thinks they are ill all the time!

There is also a lovely old folktale about borage. The story goes that if a woman wished for a proposal of marriage, she should make her lover a drink of borage to boost his courage, so he'd be brave and ask for her hand. We wonder if this ever actually worked!

AN ECZEMA EXPERIMENT

Science hasn't found any evidence to show that borage helps give courage. But it has found that it might be helpful when it comes to symptoms of eczema.

Eczema is a condition affecting the skin, which can make it dry, itchy and really painful at times. A study into the effects of borage took 32 children and separated them into two groups. One group was given vests coated with oil made from borage to wear every day for two weeks, and the other group was given non-coated vests to wear for the same amount of time. This study found that those who had worn the vests coated with borage oil saw an improvement in their eczema symptoms – much more than those who wore the normal vests!

MALLOW

WHAT DOES IT LOOK LIKE? The mallow can grow up to 2.5 m tall. Its leaves are wrinkly with five to seven lobes (segments that are round or pointed). These leaves are soft and silky to the touch, just like fabric. The mallow's flowers have five bright pinky-purple petals with a dark pinky-purple shading on the inside of each flower. The seed pods look like little cheese wheels – round with a cross in the middle and green in colour. These seed pods grow out from the stems, alongside the leaves. When you squish the branches, they leak a slimy, clear substance called **mucilage**. The mallow root is also huge and is known as a tap root.

WHERE DOES IT GROW? Once you learn to recognize mallow, you'll see it popping up in all sorts of places – through cracks in pavements, down alleyways or in wastelands and woodlands.

SCIENTIFIC NAME *Malva sylvestris*

NICKNAMES Cheeses, high mallow, tall mallow

PARTS YOU CAN EAT The whole plant is edible, apart from the stalks.

BEST TIME TO PICK IT You'll find mallow flowers and seed pods in spring and summer, when it's warmer. But the leaves can be found pretty much all year long!

THE FORAGER'S DICTIONARY
MUCILAGE

It sounds like a type of slime a ghost would leave on a wall, right? Well, it is slime, but it's not from ghosts . . . It's a slime that naturally fills most plants.

WHAT CAN YOU DO WITH IT?
Wild cheese wheel, anyone?

The mallow is one of the best wild foods you can find. Its flowers are soft and sweet, but the seed pod is the best bit. These pods are known as cheese wheels because they look like little round wheels of cheese. When the weather gets warmer, in late spring and summer, the pods become a ripe green colour – this is when they're ready to eat. They make for a refreshing cucumber-flavoured snack that pops with flavour!

Colour-changing jam

Not many people know that jam can be made from flowers. And what's really cool about making jam with mallow flowers is that they turn the jam bright blue! You can either leave the jam blue or add a bit of lemon juice while it's cooking and watch as the blue colour turns pink.

FORAGER'S CHALLENGE
1. Find and identify a mallow plant.
2. Eat one of the mallow cheese wheels!

I DIDN'T KNOW THAT!

DOES MARSHMALLOW COME FROM MALLOWS?

The answer to this is yes (well – sort of!). We owe the creation of that soft, fluffy treat to the family of mallow plants called Malvaceae – which the mallow is a part of. Ancient Egyptians were the first to create a type of marshmallow by stirring honey and sap from a plant in the mallow family together to create a sweet, gloopy treat. They considered it so special that it was reserved for gods and royalty only.

HEALTHY FATS?

The mallow is really good for us as it is packed full of great things, including calcium, iron, potassium, protein and fibre. It also contains healthy fats omega-3 and omega-6. If mallow was a Pokémon card, it would definitely be one of those rare shiny ones!

TAP TAP

A tap root is a huge root that grows down deep into the earth. These roots are special because they draw up the nutrients from deep in the soil that would otherwise be left 'untapped' – similar to how your water tap works at home. When the plant dies, it releases all this goodness back into the top layer of the soil. This then benefits all the other plants and trees that grow in that area. The circle of life strikes again!

SOOTHING CHEWS

Many ancient civilizations – including the Romans and Europeans – valued the mallow for its uses in medicine. What makes the mallow so special is the slimy mucilage inside. This gooey substance was used in the same way we use the aloe vera plant today. Because it is cooling and soothing, the mallow's slime was great for calming burns, sores and skin issues such as eczema.

Tea, syrup or cough sweets would also be made from the plant in order to soothe coughs. The idea behind this is that when a mallow-made substance is drunk or eaten, the mucilage forms a soothing protective film over our mucous membrane – which lines our nose, mouth and lungs – and helps to stop our coughs hurting so much.

In the olden days, mallow was also given to teething babies to chew on, much in the same way teething rings are used today. This was because it was believed to be satisfying to chew and soothing for the baby's gums.

A GIFT FROM THE GODS

Mallow does crop up quite a bit in the history books. A plant as delicious and nutritious as mallow was always going to get a lot of attention from our ancestors! They loved it because it was good to eat and they thought it was useful for healing painful wounds. In fact, they loved it so much they believed the mallow was proof that the gods had our best intentions at heart. Why else would they have given us such an awesome plant?

The mallow mucilage was also once considered to have great magical powers. In folklore, it was said that the slimy sap from mallow could protect you from fire – and even repel witches!

Some ancient records state that mallow was once planted on top of graves because it was believed to feed the dead buried below. Others thought that mallow seeds placed on the eyes of the dead had the power to drive out evil spirits . . . and might even open the gates of paradise!

SWEET VIOLET

WHAT DOES IT LOOK LIKE?
It's easy to spot sweet violets because their bright violet colour catches the eye – though only when they flower, in late winter and early spring. They also smell wonderful. The flowers are quite small and have five petals, two at the top and three at the bottom, creating a shape like an X. The bottom centre petal overlaps the X, poking out and down and making it look like the violet is sticking out its tongue.

Most of the time, sweet violets growing in the wild are purple, but every now and then you might get lucky and find pure white ones. The leaves are a deep green colour and heart-shaped with toothed (jagged) edges. They are also what's known as **perennial**.

WHERE DOES IT GROW?
Sweet violets grow in woodlands, along pathways and under hedgerows.

SCIENTIFIC NAME
Viola odorata

NICKNAMES
English violet, wood violet, florist's violet, heart's ease

PARTS YOU CAN EAT
Leaves and flowers

BEST TIME TO PICK IT
Sweet violets make an appearance in late winter and early spring.

THE FORAGER'S DICTIONARY
PERENNIAL
Sweet violets are what's called a perennial. This means the plant lives and flowers for more than two years. So if you find a great big patch of sweet violets, you can return to the same place year after year to collect its flowers and leaves.

WHAT CAN YOU DO WITH IT?

Decorate cakes and puddings

Traditionally, sweet violets were collected to celebrate the arrival of spring. The flowers are most commonly used as they come or crystallized in sugar to decorate sweet treats. Their beautiful colours make desserts and cakes look pretty.

I DIDN'T KNOW THAT!

THEY STOP US SMELLING

No, not like that! You still need to have a bath occasionally. Sweet violets smell amazing, but weirdly, we can't enjoy these sweet scents for long. Why? Because sweet violets contain a chemical that temporarily shuts off the smell receptors in our noses. This means the more we smell the flowers, the less well we can smell! You can test this yourself when you find some. Take a sniff and enjoy the first whiff of perfume, then take more sniffs and notice how the scent appears to fade away.

THEY MAKE THINGS CHANGE COLOUR

If you make yourself a bottle of sweet-violet syrup or a cup of sweet-violet tea, you'll be amazed by just how bright blue the tea or syrup turns. Now take your tea or syrup and add a few drops of fresh lemon juice, and watch as the colour changes from blue to bright pink!

What sorcery is this?! Well this happens because when we add an acid such as lemon juice to a sweet violet recipe, it changes something called the pH of the liquid. You might have heard of pH in science lessons, but don't worry if not, it doesn't matter (and the sweet violet won't mind). All you need to know is that it's this change in pH that affects the colours we see in the syrup or tea.

FORAGER'S CHALLENGE

1. Find and identify some sweet-violet flowers.

2. Make a bright blue violet tea then add a few drops of lemon juice and watch the colour transform.

EASE YOUR WAY TO SWEET SLEEP

Sweet violets, often called heart's ease, have been used to make people sleepy and bring a sense of calm since the time of the ancient Greeks. This peaceful feeling was useful for soothing things such as headaches or to help people when they felt sad or couldn't sleep. Tea made with the flowers was also used as a gargle, like mouthwash, and was said to help heal sore mouths and throat infections.

Any plant that's said to have sleepy effects tends to attract the eye of scientists. This is because plants that make us feel calm can be really good for our mental health, helping us to feel peaceful when we might be nervous or worried. When scientists studied the flowers to see if they had any positive health benefits, they found that sweet violets can soothe headaches, help people to sleep, heal dry coughs and are full of important antioxidants, which keep us healthy.

ZEUS AND IO

The ancient Greeks adored sweet violets so much they'd make crowns from the flowers. These crowns weren't worn just because they looked awesome – the Greeks believed that by wearing the crown it would relieve their headaches, help them to sleep and also give them pleasant dreams.

There is a Greek myth about sweet violets. The story goes that once upon a time, Zeus, the ancient Greek god of the sky and thunder, fell in love with a princess named Io. But Zeus was married. When his wife, the goddess Hera, became suspicious of her husband, Zeus turned Io into a cow to hide her and protect himself. As if that wasn't bad enough, Hera then sent a gadfly (a biting insect that especially nibbles on cows and horses) to sting and bother Io, so she had to wander far from home. It's said that Zeus felt really sorry for what had happened (and so he should), so he made sweet violets grow from Io's tears – which at least meant she had something nice to eat!

SELF-HEAL

WHAT DOES IT LOOK LIKE?
This small but mighty plant has a square stem. Roll the stem round in your fingers to feel it! Moving up the stem, the **opposite leaves** are green, long and oval-shaped. The area where flowers grow is cone-shaped and a dark shade of reddish brown. Little flowers bloom in this area at different times during the warmer months. These flowers are purple and shaped like an open mouth poking out its tongue.

WHERE DOES IT GROW?
You'll often find self-heal popping up in fields, gardens, pathways and meadows.

SCIENTIFIC NAME
Prunella vulgaris

NICKNAMES
Heal-all, carpenter's herb, heart of the earth

PARTS YOU CAN EAT
Leaves, stem and flowers

BEST TIME TO PICK IT
It blooms most abundantly in summer and early autumn.

WHAT CAN YOU DO WITH IT?

Make a salad
Self-heal leaves taste similar to lettuce, so they're nice on their own, in a sandwich or added to a salad or omelette. Some people like to blend a few leaves into their smoothies to add a bit of extra goodness.

Anyone fancy a cuppa?
Chopped self-heal leaves make a tasty last-minute addition to soups and stews, and are normally added to these dishes just before they're served. Self-heal can also be dried and used to make a powerful medicinal tea.

THE FORAGER'S DICTIONARY
OPPOSITE LEAVES
When leaves are described as being opposite, this means that two leaves are attached to the same part of a stem, but grow on opposite sides to each other.

I DIDN'T KNOW THAT!

PLANTS KNOW BEST!

Some people believe that if self-heal grows in your garden, this means the plant has come to visit you! And the reason for the visit? Because you may be in need of the self-heal's medicinal qualities...

FEED THE BEES

Bees do a lot for us, from pollinating plants to making honey. In fact, we'd be lost without them. If you'd like to say 'Thanks!' to the bees for all their hard work, then this flower makes a great gift. Self-heal is one of the honey bee's favourite flowers because of its rich nectar. So, by growing or allowing self-heal to grow in your garden, you can help promote biodiversity and support your local bees.

CARPENTER'S CURE

Self-heal has long been used by carpenters. Their job involves cutting and sawing wood all day – and, of course, they sometimes accidentally cut themselves! In the past, when this happened, carpenters would apply self-heal to their skin to stop the wound bleeding. It was also thought to clean the wound and help it heal faster. It's because of this that self-heal is known as carpenter's herb.

FORAGER'S CHALLENGE

1. Find and identify a self-heal flower.

2. Roll it in your fingers to feel its unique square stem.

AN ESSENTIAL HERB

Self-heal ... it's a good name, isn't it? If we asked you, 'What do you think a plant called self-heal is good for?', what would you say? Probably that it has something to do with healing! Even its Latin name, *Prunella*, comes from the German word for quinsy, which is a severe sore throat that self-heal is supposed to be able to cure.

It's most commonly used in herbal medicine, like tea, to treat things such as heart disease, stomach issues, sore throats, mouth ulcers, viral infections and tumours. Indeed, self-heal has such a long list of uses in traditional medicine that it is still considered by many herbalists to be an essential part of their herbal medicine cabinet.

DRUIDIC RITUAL

A Druid was a leader who had an important role in the religion, law, stories and medicine of the Celtic people (who lived over 2,000 years ago). One of their jobs was collecting medicinal herbs. Folklore has it that the head Druid used to harvest self-heal plants at night, when the Moon was at that phase in the month when it can't be seen. The head Druid would use a special golden sickle (a curved cutting tool) to harvest the plant, and then hold the leaves above their head in their left hand.

We can't be sure of the details though because the Druids didn't write anything down. Most written accounts we have of them come from the invading Romans, who hated them and mostly said bad things, so we can't totally trust their version of who the Druids were. When we look back on history today, it's more likely that they were experts in using plants for medicine and lived in harmony with nature. The Romans probably didn't like them simply because they wouldn't do what they were told!

RED CLOVER

WHAT DOES IT LOOK LIKE? The flower heads are round, and look a bit like the end of a spear. They are normally bright pink or red in colour. On each flower's stem, there are three leaves – called a **trifoliate** – which are small, green and oval-shaped. They grow close to the ground, so make sure you're looking down when trying to find them!

WHERE DOES IT GROW? Red clover likes to grow in towns and gardens, grasslands, pathways, parks and fields.

SCIENTIFIC NAME *Trifolium pratense*

NICKNAMES Trefoil, pink clover, shamrock

PARTS YOU CAN EAT Flowers, seeds and leaves

BEST TIME TO PICK IT Red clover can be picked from spring all the way through to autumn.

WHAT CAN YOU DO WITH IT?
Pink clover lemonade
As well as being tasty on its own, red clover can be made into a delicious, sweet cordial drink which can look a glorious pink!

THE FORAGER'S DICTIONARY
TRIFOLIATE

A red clover's leaves grow in what's called a trifoliate. This simply means it has three leaves. Though if you're lucky, you can find yourself a rare four-leaf, or sometimes five- or six-leaf clover!

I DIDN'T KNOW THAT!

A LUCKY CHARM?

You might have heard that it's lucky to find a four-leaf clover. In fact, the chances of finding a four-leaf clover are about 1 in 5,000. There is even a world record for the number of four-leaf clovers collected in an hour, set by a ten-year-old American called Katie Borka, who found 166 on 23 June 2018! Now that's lucky.

A HELPFUL WEED INDEED

Red clover is often called a noxious weed. Sounds like something bad or gross, right? But just like the dandelion, the red clover isn't a baddie, it's a goodie! Weeds are here for a reason. Red clover – when left alone and not sprayed with weed killer – actually makes the soil a better place for plants to grow. It also supports a wide range of wildlife and is especially loved by bees.

FORAGER'S CHALLENGE

1. Find and identify a red clover.

2. Find a lucky four-leaf clover!

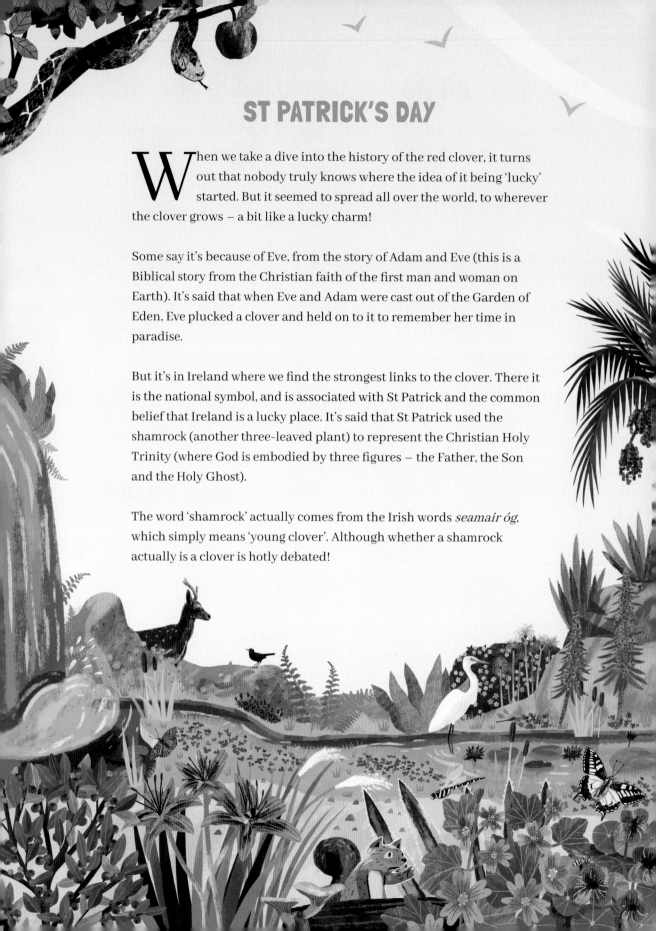

ST PATRICK'S DAY

When we take a dive into the history of the red clover, it turns out that nobody truly knows where the idea of it being 'lucky' started. But it seemed to spread all over the world, to wherever the clover grows – a bit like a lucky charm!

Some say it's because of Eve, from the story of Adam and Eve (this is a Biblical story from the Christian faith of the first man and woman on Earth). It's said that when Eve and Adam were cast out of the Garden of Eden, Eve plucked a clover and held on to it to remember her time in paradise.

But it's in Ireland where we find the strongest links to the clover. There it is the national symbol, and is associated with St Patrick and the common belief that Ireland is a lucky place. It's said that St Patrick used the shamrock (another three-leaved plant) to represent the Christian Holy Trinity (where God is embodied by three figures – the Father, the Son and the Holy Ghost).

The word 'shamrock' actually comes from the Irish words *seamair óg*, which simply means 'young clover'. Although whether a shamrock actually is a clover is hotly debated!

NOT JUST A LUCKY CHARM

For years, the red clover has been seen as a very special flower – not only because of its associations with good luck, but because it was believed to be able to help us in our everyday lives.

In Europe, the plant has long been used for the treatment of the menopause. This is a stage in a woman's life when the menstrual cycles of her body change as she gets older. The red clover can be made into a tea to help reduce the uncomfortable symptoms of menopause, including changes in body temperature. The flower is also used for other illnesses, such as asthma and arthritis.

PRIMROSE

WHAT DOES IT LOOK LIKE? Primrose flowers are a pale yellow and white colour with five petals, which fade into a darker shade of yellow towards the centre. The leaves are dark green and wrinkly, forming a rosette (ring) at the plant's base. The stem is hairy and can be a shade of reddish green with one single flower on top. The plants are special because they are what's called **actinomorphic**, and they also smell lovely. Give one a sniff – it has a delightful floral scent.

THE FORAGER'S DICTIONARY

ACTINOMORPHIC

Primrose flowers are what's called actinomorphic. This means they can be divided into three or more identical sections. Another way to think about it is if you put a mirror in the middle of a primrose flower, you would see exactly the same flower reflected on both sides of the mirror.

WHERE DOES IT GROW? Primroses grow wild in woodland clearings or on grassy banks. Wild ones can be rare in some places, where their habitats have been destroyed.

SCIENTIFIC NAME *Primula vulgaris*

NICKNAMES English primrose

PARTS YOU CAN EAT Flowers and leaves

BEST TIME TO PICK IT Primroses grow all year round and blossom in late winter and spring.

WHAT CAN YOU DO WITH IT?

Make desserts

Primrose flowers are most commonly used as pretty cake decorations or cooked and used in puddings or mousses. You can also turn them into jam or syrup, so you can enjoy the scent of the flower all year round. Sweet!

Brew floral tea

If you love the smell of primrose flowers, pop a few in some hot water to make a nice floral-flavoured cup of tea. You could even add a teaspoon of home-made primrose syrup!

Give your teeth a workout

When you munch a fresh primrose flower, it has a unique chompy, chunky texture that makes it satisfying to eat.

I DIDN'T KNOW THAT!

A RARE WEED INDEED

There used to be far more wild primroses in the UK than there are now. But don't worry, the flower isn't in danger of going extinct. It can still be found growing wild in loads of places – in fact, it grows so well in some regions that it's considered a weed. If you live somewhere they are rare, though, make sure you only pick a few from a big patch, so they don't become even rarer.

EARLY BLOOMERS

The primrose is an early-blooming flower, meaning its flowers appear before lots of other plants burst into bloom. In fact, its name comes from the Latin *prima rosa* which means 'first rose'! You may even get lucky and find it flowering towards the end of winter.

FORAGER'S CHALLENGE

1. Find and identify a primrose.

2. Try decorating a cake with some primrose flowers.

BREATHE EASY

In traditional herbalism, primrose flowers were used in the same way as daisies. It's said that the flowers can make us feel calmer, less worried and less nervous. Tea made with primroses is said to be good for lots of other things, too, such as easing headaches and helping to clear chesty coughs. Balms and salves would also be infused with the flowers and used to help heal wounds or soothe aches, strains and pains.

When scientists had a good look at the primrose, they found that the plant has antibacterial properties, meaning it can help fight bacteria that cause infections. They also found that when it was combined with a few other plants (a herb called thyme, for instance), it could indeed help ease coughs and shortness of breath.

PORTALS TO THE FAIRY WORLD

Primroses are planted in gardens these days because they look beautiful and bloom early, bringing a splash of colour to our flower beds. But not so long ago they were planted in gardens for quite different reasons. In folklore, primrose flowers have a strong link with fairies. It was believed that if you put a primrose flower outside your home this would make passing fairies happy, and they might even bless your house (if you were lucky!). It was also said that if you were to eat the flower of a primrose, soon you would see a fairy with your very own eyes . . .

But the fairy magic doesn't end there. The Celts believed that a patch of primroses found growing in the wild was a sign that you had found a gateway to the fairy realm. It was said that if a posy (a little bundle of flowers) made of primroses was touched to the surface of a rock, a portal to the fairy world would open.

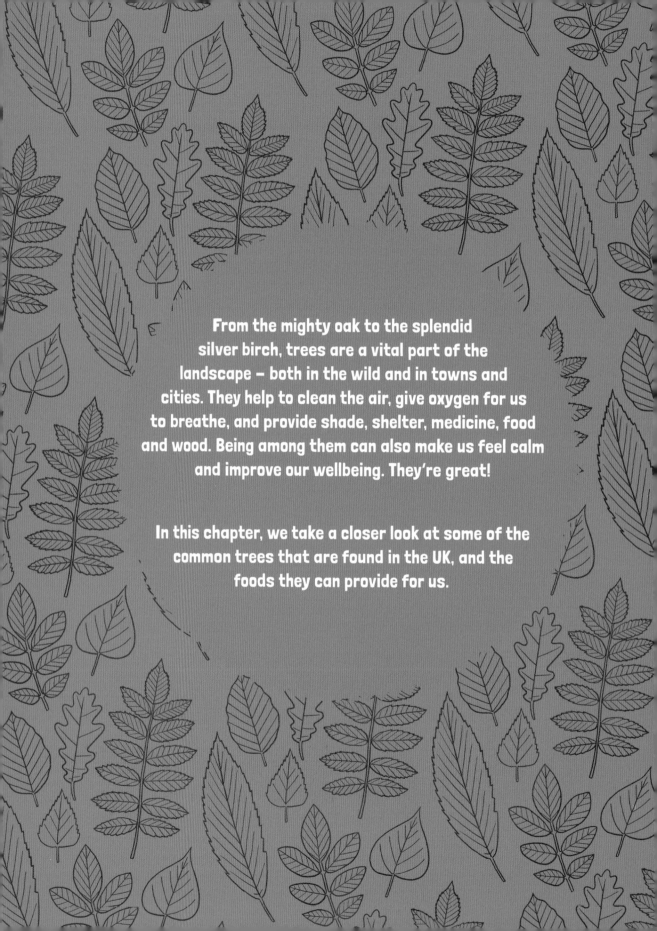

From the mighty oak to the splendid
silver birch, trees are a vital part of the
landscape – both in the wild and in towns and
cities. They help to clean the air, give oxygen for us
to breathe, and provide shade, shelter, medicine, food
and wood. Being among them can also make us feel calm
and improve our wellbeing. They're great!

In this chapter, we take a closer look at some of the
common trees that are found in the UK, and the
foods they can provide for us.

TREES

BEECH

WHAT DOES IT LOOK LIKE? The beech tree is known as a woodland giant because it can reach up to 45 m in height! Its trunk grows in a unique way and looks like it's almost sculpted in clay. Its bark is a smooth shade of grey and shines almost silver in the sunlight. Its leaves are oval-shaped with a point at the tip, and in early spring they are almost translucent (which means they allow light through). These young leaves also have a line of fur around the outside and appear **wavy** rather than toothed. The beechnuts, which appear in autumn, are covered in a spiky, triangular, brown husk that's hard to open. Each husk contains one or sometimes two or even three beechnuts.

WHERE DOES IT GROW? Beech trees grow in parks, woodlands and forests.

SCIENTIFIC NAME *Fagus sylvatica*

NICKNAMES The queen of trees

HOW LONG DOES IT LIVE FOR? Beech trees can live for up to 400 years!

PARTS YOU CAN EAT Young leaves and beechnuts

BEST TIME TO PICK IT You can eat the
leaves in early spring and the beechnuts in autumn.

WHAT CAN YOU DO WITH IT?

Eat your greens!

In early spring, beech leaves are a fresh green colour, and their texture is nice and soft and tender at this time of the year, too. They have a plain but refreshing flavour that works well in salads. They can also be made into a tea.

Beech roasted

Beechnuts can be eaten raw in autumn but they don't taste very nice. What's more, some people say that eating too many can cause tummy upset. Not everyone agrees with this – it all comes down to each person's food sensitivity. Just to be safe, though, if you wish to eat large quantities of beechnuts, then it's worth processing them first. To do this, simply roast them in a pan for around 5 minutes until they give off a delicious toasty smell **(ask your adult for help with this!)**. You can then grind the roasted nuts into a flour, pesto or paste – or squeeze them to extract a delicious oil, which people use to stay healthy.

THE FORAGER'S DICTIONARY

WAVY

When leaves are described as wavy, this means the outside of the leaf isn't flat but has waves, like the sea (or maybe like your grandparents' frilly curtains!).

I DIDN'T KNOW THAT!

WAR COFFEE

Roasted beechnuts (along with acorns and the roots of a plant called chicory) were made into a popular coffee-type drink in the Second World War, when things like real coffee were really hard to get. Soldiers and civilians must have had to become master foragers during these difficult times, when there wasn't so much regular food.

BODGE JOBS

Have you ever heard the term 'bodge job'? This is what we say today to describe when someone has fixed something quickly and not very well. Like if a chair leg falls off and you fix it back on with bubblegum! This use of the term is actually a bit odd, though, since bodgers were master furniture makers, who would walk into the forest with nothing but tools and come back out with finely made furniture. And guess what wood they used to do this? Beech wood!

FORAGER'S CHALLENGE

1. Find and identify a beech tree.
2. Eat some soft, fresh beech leaves in early spring.

TRUFFLE TREASURE TROVE

Truffles are edible fungi (a group of organisms that includes moulds, yeast, mushrooms, and toadstools) that grow underground among the roots of certain trees – oak, hazel and beech. Truffles are considered to be one of the most delicious foods in the world. Foragers have to use their expert knowledge to find wild ones at certain times of the year. This makes them very valuable. The most expensive truffle ever sold went for more than £30,000!

STOP THAT COUGH!

Many parts of the beech tree were used for medicine in ancient Europe. People would pick the leaves, cook them until they were squishy and then place them on parts of the body that hurt, to help ease the pain. If you had a headache, you'd put the squish on your head; if you had a painful boil, you'd cover it in beech-leaf squish. They'd also drink beech-leaf tea when they had a cough or cold.

When scientists took a careful look at the beech tree, they found that the tree's bark contained a special thing called 'antitussive agents'. Antitussives are cough suppressants that decrease the sensitivity of cough receptors in the brain, meaning you cough less. So, it seems the ancient Europeans were on to something!

BEECH BOOKS

Did you know that the beech tree played a major role in creating the very thing you're holding in your hands right now? Books! Early 'books', or writing tablets, were made from thinly sliced beech wood (or strips of birch bark). People would carve their writing into these soft wood slices.

In fact, some experts think the word 'book' comes from the old word for 'beech', though others say it comes from 'birch'. Either way, beech wood was also later used to make covers for books with paper pages. The thin slices of wood or 'book boards' would help to protect and support the pages inside.

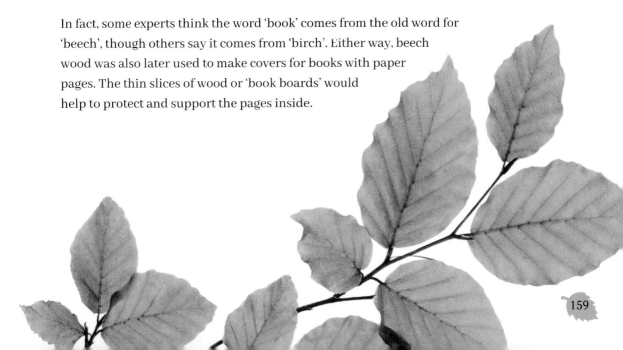

SILVER BIRCH

WHAT DOES IT LOOK LIKE? You can't miss the silver birch tree because its bark is a bright shade of white. When you look closely at this bark, you can see it's covered in little horizontal markings. Unlike most trees, silver birch bark peels like paper – just feel for an edge by one of the horizontal lines and pull gently. If you peel back some of the bark, you'll see something called the **cambium layer**, which is pale green or white, but might sometimes look orange if it has been exposed to light and air. A silver birch can grow up to around 30 m in height in some conditions. Its leaves are oval – or triangle-shaped with serrated edges.

WHERE DOES IT GROW? You'll find it most commonly growing in woodland and forests.

SCIENTIFIC NAME *Betula pendula*

NICKNAMES White birch, warty birch, European white birch, East Asian white birch

HOW LONG DOES IT LIVE FOR? Between around 60 and 140 years

PARTS YOU CAN EAT Leaves, sap, cambium layer

THE FORAGER'S DICTIONARY
CAMBIUM LAYER

The cambium layer is the third layer down within a tree. The outside of the tree's bark is called the outer bark, and this protects the tree like a shield. Next up is the inner bark, which is where food and nutrients are passed through the tree. Finally, there's the cambium layer, which is the part of the trunk that actually grows and produces more bark and wood.

BEST TIME TO PICK IT The sap and leaves are fresh in early spring. The cambium layer is available all year round.

WHAT CAN YOU DO WITH IT?
Survival food

The cambium layer is edible and has long been used as a survival food. People lost in the woods could find a birch tree and, using a knife, cut off some of the thin, pale green cambium layer that lies between the bark and the wood. The cambium can be eaten raw but is nicer cooked. It can also be dried and ground to make flour. **Only try this with an adult who knows how to get the cambium out safely and without harming the tree!**

Make instant paper

Today, trees are cut down to make paper. But in a time before paper was readily available, many ancient cultures would simply peel off some birch bark in long sheets and write and draw on it.

161

I DIDN'T KNOW THAT!

EVERY PART IS USEFUL

Because birch wood is so strong and waterproof, ancient people would use it to make all sorts of things. The birch trunk would be hollowed out to make canoes or household items such as cups. Other parts of the tree could be used to make dyes, glues and oil.

TAP THE SAP

Each year in early spring (around March in the UK), the birch tree sends all the sap it has kept safely stored in its roots up its trunk and branches, to help it grow healthy leaves. **You mustn't try this yourself**, but if you're with a sap-finding expert (and if you find a tree big enough that it can spare a little sap), you can enjoy a tasty mineral-rich drink.

WOODPECKERS LOVE SILVER BIRCHES

Many nesting birds like to make the birch tree their home, especially the woodpecker.

A SPECIAL TYPE OF FUNGUS

A special type of mushroom called chaga grows on birch trees. This mushroom is said to have many powerful medicinal properties. **Experts are still unsure whether chaga is safe to eat though, so it's very important you don't try it!**

FORAGER'S CHALLENGE

1. Find and identify a silver birch tree.

2. Peel off a piece of the papery bark and try drawing on it.

NATURE'S PAINKILLER

The silver birch tree is famous for its powers to help heal our bodies. People have used it for thousands of years in lots of different places around the world to treat pain and headaches, just like how we use medicine today. They did this by making and drinking tea, using the leaves to help heal cuts, or using the bark to splint (support) broken bones.

Today, people still use the birch tree to make things that help our skin and bodies. A gel made from birch-tree bark has been created recently to help heal small cuts and wounds. Birch sap is used in many beauty products because it helps our skin stay hydrated and healthy. Birch also contains antioxidants, which are good for our bodies.

THE OLD MAN AND THE BIRCH TREE

If you look at the bark of a birch tree, you'll see it's covered in horizontal markings. But why does it have these marks? There is an incredible tale that tells the story of the birch-tree markings. This was recorded in writing by Frank Linderman in his book *Indian Why Stories*, as told to him by an elder of the Blackfeet Nation, a tribe of Indigenous Americans.

One summer, long ago, the old man became all hot and bothered on account of the great heat. To try to find some cooler air, he travelled to the top of the tallest hill and then to the lowest river, but neither offered any relief.

In despair, the old man called to the winds to send
a breeze to cool him down. The winds responded, but it
wasn't enough for the old man. He next asked the winds to
blow hard enough to push all the hot air from the world. The winds
tried, but still it wasn't enough. So, in a rage, the old man called upon
the winds to blow down a fir tree, a pine tree, a spruce tree and a birch
tree. He also ordered the trees to bend and snap. This they did – all except
for the birch tree, which refused to break, even though it bent right down to
the ground.

This made the old man even more furious, so he told the winds to blow even
harder. But still the birch tree didn't break. Instead, it replied, 'I will never
break for any wind. I will bend but I shall never break'. At this point the
old man got very angry indeed. He took out his knife and ran to the
birch tree, slashing the tree's bark from top to bottom, giving it the
marks we can see to this day.

COMMON OAK

WHAT DOES IT LOOK LIKE?
The common oak grows to around 20 to 40 m tall – that's pretty big! Its bark is a grey colour and deeply **fissured**. Its leaves are green and distinctive with their four or five deep lobes and smooth edges. The oak has male and female flowers, which grow on separate parts of the tree. The female flowers are tiny, but the male ones grow into long yellow catkins (you can find out more about these on page 174). The acorns, which are the oak's nuts, have two main parts. The first is the cupule (the acorn's cap) and the other is the pericarp (the hard outer shell). Together, these two parts look like a seed wearing a nice little hat. The acorn ripens from green to brown before it loosens from the cupule and falls to the ground, which happens in autumn.

WHERE DOES IT GROW?
The mighty oak tree loves to grow tall and strong in woodlands and forests. You'll also be able to find it in parks up and down the country.

SCIENTIFIC NAME *Quercus robur*

NICKNAMES English oak, pedunculate oak

HOW LONG DOES IT LIVE FOR?
From 100 to over 1,000 years!

THE FORAGER'S DICTIONARY
FISSURED
When a tree's bark is described as fissured, this means it has cracks and deep splits.

PARTS YOU CAN EAT You can eat the acorns once they have been processed (read on for more about this!).

BEST TIME TO PICK IT The acorns are ripe when they turn brown and fall to the ground in autumn.

WHAT CAN YOU DO WITH IT?
Grind 'em up and eat 'em

Packed with healthy fats, protein, carbohydrates, fibre and loads of vitamins and minerals, acorns are great for our health. BUT . . . you can't just eat an acorn straight off the floor. Not only will it taste disgusting, but it won't be very good for you. Acorns have to be processed before they can be eaten. See below to learn how – it's super simple. Once they've been processed, acorns can be roasted and nibbed as a nice snack or ground to make a free coffee alternative (like beechnuts) or flour. People have been eating acorns in this way for thousands of years, especially acorn flour, which was used for making bread, pasta and even cookies.

HOW TO PROCESS ACORNS

METHOD 1

1. Remove the acorns from their shells using a nutcracker.

2. Place the acorns in a pan and add water to twice the depth of the acorns.

3. Boil the water for about 15 minutes. It will turn brown, as something called tannins are released from the acorns.

4. Pour away the water and repeat steps 2 and 3 until the water stays clear when the acorns are boiled.

METHOD 2

1. Shell the acorns as described above.

2. Place the acorns in a pan and add hot or cold water to twice the depth of the acorns.

3. Instead of boiling the water, just leave the acorns to soak until the water turns brown.

4. Pour away the water and repeat steps 2 and 3 until the water stays clear.

I DIDN'T KNOW THAT!

FOOD AND SHELTER

The oak tree supports more life in the UK than any other tree in the country. Its leaves are eaten by caterpillars, and its acorns are harvested by mammals such as squirrels and badgers. Even its fallen leaves provide food and shelter for things such as caterpillars and beetles. When they rot down, the leaves release nutrients into the soil, making it more fertile, which means it's easier for things to grow.

IT'S A SURVIVOR

The oak is one of the oldest trees on the planet – it's been here way longer than us humans! It's thought that the first oak trees may have popped up more than 55 million years ago. Unlike the dinosaurs, oak trees haven't gone extinct and have survived many changes in the Earth's climate.

FORAGER'S CHALLENGE

1. Find and identify an oak tree.

2. Visit an oak in autumn and draw a little face on an acorn. You can even make a body out of twigs and join it to your acorn to create a cool figure.

BARKING UP THE RIGHT TREE!

Oaks have provided people with both food and medicine for as long as humans have been around. The parts of the tree used for healing people were the inner bark, leaves and acorns. These have something that's known as 'natural astringency'. An astringent is a chemical that shrinks or constricts (tightens) body tissues, which can help stop bleeding and diarrhoea – though some studies have shown that astringents could do more harm than good if not used in the right way!

Not surprisingly, scientists wanted to take a closer look at these claims, and what they found backed up what the herbalists had been saying for hundreds of years! In addition, one study discovered that oak extract could help to improve our mood, give us energy and help us sleep.

THE STORY OF THE OAK KING AND THE HOLLY KING

In many ancient traditions, there is an epic tale about a great, endless battle between two tree kings – the Oak King and the Holly King. The story goes that these two powerful tree kings were brothers who met to do battle twice each year to decide who would rule over the seasons. The first battle happened on the day of the summer solstice, when the Holly King was weak and the Oak King was strong. The Oak King would always win that battle and rule over the forests until late summer. Then, on the winter solstice, the Holly King would come back, strong and ready to fight. He in turn would always win that battle and become the ruler of the forests until the following spring.

The two trees were said to represent the seasons, and this mythical story was a way to explain the seasonal cycles of the year.

WALNUT

WHAT DOES IT LOOK LIKE? Walnut trees grow to around 35 m in height. They have a short trunk with smooth bark that's brown in colour when the tree is young but fades to grey as it ages. Its leaves are a shiny green colour with five to nine oval **paired leaflets** and one **terminal leaflet**. The fruits that contain the walnuts are a fleshy green or brown colour with tiny white dots. Be careful when opening these shells as they can stain skin and clothes. The walnuts themselves look like little brains.

WHERE DOES IT GROW? Walnut trees tend to grow around parks and fields, along the sides of pathways and sometimes in woodlands.

SCIENTIFIC NAME *Juglans regia* (common walnut), *Juglans nigra* (black walnut)

NICKNAMES Common walnut, English walnut, black walnut

HOW LONG DOES IT LIVE FOR? Around 100 to 200 years

PARTS YOU CAN EAT Walnuts!

BEST TIME TO PICK IT The unripe walnut husks can be picked in summer. The husks open in autumn, dropping their ripe walnuts to the ground.

WHAT CAN YOU DO WITH IT?
Fruits of the forest
The fleshy green fruits (called husks or shells) can be collected in late summer, before the walnut has fully formed inside. If you cut the fruit open early it should be soft and white inside, and it has a sort of citrussy smell. They aren't all that nice to eat fresh, so they're usually infused into syrups, pickled or made into a special walnut ketchup!

Wet or dry
When the walnuts are fully formed and ripe in autumn, you can eat them raw, either as something called 'wet walnuts', which are straight from the husk, or 'dried walnuts', which is how they are more commonly eaten. To dry them (they keep much better if they're dried and can be used in more ways), simply crack open the husks, spread them out in a well-ventilated place, but away from direct sunlight, and let them dry naturally. This should take around two weeks. They can then be eaten as they are, roasted, added to all sorts of recipes or boiled to make a drink.

THE FORAGER'S DICTIONARY
PAIRED AND TERMINAL LEAFLETS

Paired leaflets are smallish leaves that grow opposite each other across the stem of the leaf (called a rachis). The terminal leaflet grows all on its own at the end of a stem or branch.

I DIDN'T KNOW THAT!

TREE TWINS

There are two types of walnut tree in the UK: the English walnut and the black walnut. Both look really similar and both have edible walnuts. You can tell the difference between them by the colour of their walnut shells. English walnuts have lighter shells while black walnut shells are much darker.

WOOD-WIDE HACKER

Yes, you read that right, black walnut trees are similar to computer hackers! It's believed that all trees are connected to an underground fungal network that we call the 'wood wide web'. Just like the internet, the trees use this network to send each other messages and also share things such as nutrients. Most trees are very friendly and take good care of each other, but the black walnut tree seems to be an exception. It is thought that it hacks this network, steals resources and even tries to sabotage other trees!

SQUIRREL HELP

Black walnut trees might not be friendly to other trees, but they are friendly to wildlife. The leaves are eaten by caterpillars and the tree provides loads of delicious and nutritious walnuts that are enjoyed by mammals such as mice and especially squirrels! Did you know squirrels might plant millions of trees every year? They do this not because they love gardening, but because they forget where they buried their nuts (or they might have just abandoned them!). These nuts then grow into great big trees. Thanks, squirrels!

FORAGER'S CHALLENGE

1. Find and identify a walnut tree.

2. Collect some ripe walnuts in autumn and try them 'wet' and 'dried' to taste the difference.

BRAIN FOODS

The Romans loved walnut trees. They used the nuts as food, but they also believed that eating them could make them feel lovey-dovey. And the Romans weren't the only people who thought walnuts had special powers. The ancient Greeks who came before them thought walnuts could help cure inflammation and baldness.

Although it might not be true that walnuts help you get a girlfriend or boyfriend, we do now know that they're really good for our brains. Which, considering walnuts do actually look like little brains, is pretty cool! Scientists have found that walnuts can help us understand things better, and they've even been shown to improve memory and learning in mice with Alzheimer's disease (a brain disease that affects memory, behaviour and thinking).

FOOD OF THE GODS

Trees that were important to people in the past are often mentioned in stories and hinted at in names, such as the story of Narcissus and the scientific name for daffodils (see page 194). In the same way, to find the walnut's story all we have to do is translate its scientific name, *Juglans regia*, which means 'royal nut of Jupiter'.

So who exactly was Jupiter? With a little research, we find that Jupiter was the Roman god of the sky and thunder, and king of all the gods of ancient Rome. There are loads of stories about him in Roman mythology, including one that says that when he came down from the heavens and walked the Earth, he would eat only walnuts. Brainy chap! Hearing this, normal Romans thought, 'If the gods eat them, they must be good!' and they too grew, harvested and ate walnuts as much as possible. They even took walnuts with them to plant in the countries they invaded, as their empire spread across parts of the world.

SWEET CHESTNUT

WHAT DOES IT LOOK LIKE? The sweet chestnut tree can grow quite large – to around 35 m tall. Its leaves are long and glossy with an oblong shape and serrated edges, ending with a point. Its bark is a greyish-brown colour with vertical fissures (long cracks) that can sometimes twist like a pattern round the trunk. The male flowers are long yellow **catkins**. The female flowers grow at the base of these catkins, looking like tiny chestnut shells. The chestnuts that fall in autumn are a reddish-brown colour, round in shape with a flat side, and have a little tuft of hair on top. These chestnuts grow within a bright green, extremely prickly case!

WHERE DOES IT GROW? You'll mostly find sweet chestnut trees in places where people have planted them, such as in towns and gardens, hedgerows and along field edges.

SCIENTIFIC NAME *Castanea sativa*

NICKNAMES Chestnut, Spanish chestnut

HOW LONG DOES IT LIVE FOR? 700 to over 2,000 years!

PARTS YOU CAN EAT Chestnuts

BEST TIME TO PICK IT The sweet chestnuts will ripen and fall in autumn.

WHAT CAN YOU DO WITH IT?
Healthy sweets!

Naturally sweet, chestnuts are history's candy, which is why there are so many songs and traditions associated with them. It's also why they are called 'sweet chestnuts'. But there's a small catch. Although you can eat sweet chestnuts fresh when you find them, they don't taste very nice. You need to let them dry for a few days so the starches inside transform into natural sugars, which makes the chestnuts delicious and sweet.

Roasting on an open fire...

Thanks to that classic Christmas song, the most famous way to eat sweet chestnuts is after they've been roasted over an open fire. But this isn't the only way you can enjoy them: they can be candied, boiled, steamed, deep-fried, grilled, tinned or preserved in sugar or syrup. You can also make them into hummus, purée or soups or add them to salads.

THE FORAGER'S DICTIONARY
CATKINS

Catkins are long, slim male flowers that poke out or dangle from some trees. They don't look like typical flowers since they often don't have any petals. The name catkin comes from the Middle Dutch word *katteken* (which means 'kitten') because they look like little kitten's tails.

I DIDN'T KNOW THAT!

EXPLODING NUTS!

You might have heard that chestnuts can explode? Well, it's true. To stop this happening, it's very important to score the brown shells of the sweet chestnuts before you cook them. To score simply means cut an X shape in the top. This stops the pressure inside them building up to the point at which they explode!

TIME IS IN THE EYE OF THE BEHOLDER

It can take up to 25 years for the tree to start producing chestnuts. This might seem like a long time, but considering that the tree can live and provide food for wildlife and people for thousands of years, this isn't so long. Just imagine – if you plant a sweet chestnut tree today, squirrels thousands of years from now might benefit from your good deed!

FORAGER'S CHALLENGE

1. Find and identify a sweet chestnut tree.
2. Leave a chestnut out to dry then eat it and experience that sweet, nutty flavour!

BACTERIA–BUSTING LEAVES

When scientists took a look into the leaves of the sweet chestnut tree, they found something that blew their minds. Hidden within the leaves was a molecule that was new to science! This molecule is very special because it has the power to neutralize a superbug (no, not a beetle with superpowers!) known as MRSA.

Superbugs are strains of bacteria, viruses, parasites and fungi that have become resistant to antibiotics – a medicine we usually use to fight these nasty things. They are really dangerous, so a huge search for alternative antibiotics is now happening, which is leading scientists to make these amazing discoveries.

THE 100 HORSE CHESTNUT TREE

The world's oldest sweet chestnut tree is thought to be well over 2,000 years old. Confusingly, though, it's sometimes called the '100 horse chestnut tree'. The wrong number and the wrong tree?! What's going on there?

In fact, this isn't a mistake. It was called the 100 horse chestnut tree because of a legend about the Queen of Aragon and her company of 100 knights, who set out to travel to a place called Mount Etna, in Italy. Along the way, they were caught in a huge storm, so they ran to a sweet chestnut tree to seek shelter. After they left, the sweet chestnut tree was renamed the 100 horse chestnut tree – though it might have been better if had been called the '100 knight sweet chestnut tree'!

ROWAN

WHAT DOES IT LOOK LIKE?

The rowan tree grows to around 15 m in height and has smooth, silvery-brown bark with patchy markings. Its leaves are green, long and oval-shaped with toothed edges. The **hermaphrodite** flowers grow on the rowan tree in late spring or summer in dense clusters. Each flower has five creamy white petals. The berries of the rowan tree start off green then slowly fade to a bright shade of orangey-red as they get older. These berries are small, round, soft and juicy.

WHERE DOES IT GROW?
Rowan trees grow in high-up places, such as rocky mountains. But you'll also often find them growing in woodlands, parks, towns and gardens.

SCIENTIFIC NAME
Sorbus aucuparia

NICKNAMES
Mountain ash, witch wiggin tree

HOW LONG DOES IT LIVE FOR?
Around 200 years

PARTS YOU CAN EAT
You can eat the flowers and the berries, but the berries must be cooked first.

BEST TIME TO PICK IT
The blossoms appear in spring, and the berries are best in late summer or early autumn.

THE FORAGER'S DICTIONARY
HERMAPHRODITE

The rowan tree is a hermaphrodite, which means that it only has one type of flower, rather than the more usual separate male and female flowers. This single flower contains both the male and female reproductive parts, which increases the chance of successful pollination. It might sound odd, but actually this isn't uncommon in the tree world – lots of trees are hermaphrodites, including apple, plum, peach and cherry trees!

WHAT CAN YOU DO WITH IT?

Wine not

Rowan berries can make a whole host of different drinks. From wines to ales to cordials. They've even been used as a substitute for coffee.

Bitter jam

The berries are most commonly used to make what's called a 'bitter jam'. This is similar to the cranberry sauce that some people enjoy on a roast dinner. The berries are packed with loads of different vitamins and minerals, which makes this jam both delicious and nutritious!

I DIDN'T KNOW THAT!

BERRY UPSET

Rowan berries must be cooked before being eaten. This is because they contain something called parasorbic acid, which can cause stomach upsets (the seeds contain *prussic* acid, which can also be poisonous). This is nothing to worry about, as it does get broken down when the berries are heated. Us humans have to cook a lot of things before we can eat them!

THE COLDER, THE SWEETER

Rowan berries can have quite a bitter taste. But what's the reason for this bitterness? It's so that animals don't eat them, of course! Similar to rosehips, rowan berries get sweeter once the cold weather arrives.

EAT THE RAINBOW!

Rowan berries are a beautiful, vibrant red. Bright colours in natural foods don't only look amazing, they are really good or us. You see, what makes rowan berries red is carotenoids. This is something known as a pigment, and it makes the yellows, oranges and red colours we see in fruits and veggies such as pumpkins, tomatoes, sweet potatoes and carrots. Carotenoids are important for our health because they act as antioxidants, which help protect our cells from damage caused by harmful molecules.

FORAGER'S CHALLENGE
1. Find and identify a rowan tree.
2. Sit under a rowan tree covered in berries and quietly watch the birds for 10 whole minutes.

A SPOONFUL OF SUGAR HELPS
THE MEDICINE GO DOWN!

Rowan berry jam is used today as a traditional sauce that's served with things such as cheese and roast dinners. But this jam was originally used to help treat and soothe stomach issues. Turning the berries into bittersweet jam was a way to kill two birds with one stone: because the berries had to be cooked, it made them edible, and the jam could also be kept for ages. It's pretty tasty, too!

The berries were also made into infusions that were used to help treat sore throats and swollen tonsils, and to reduce inflammation of the respiratory tract (the system in your body that helps you breathe).

THE VIKING TREE

The rowan tree was very important in Norse mythology and folklore. Sacred to the ancient Norse people (who lived in Scandinavia more than a thousand years ago), the tree was often linked to powerful gods and goddesses.

Thor was the Norse god of thunder and lightning. According to Norse legend, he once grabbed an overhanging branch of a rowan tree while trying to cross a particularly dangerous river. The tree saved Thor from being dragged into the Underworld!

In places around the world, the tree is seen as a symbol of protection, particularly against witchcraft and enchantment. Today, you can still find rowan trees growing next to homes out in the remote countryside, offering shelter and safety.

LILAC

WHAT DOES IT LOOK LIKE?
The lilac tree can grow to around 6 or 7 m tall. It's most easily recognized in spring when it produces bright, fragrant flowers. These flowers grow in long, cone-shaped clusters around 10 to 20 cm in size. They are most commonly a bright shade of purple or pink but can also be white. The bark, when it's young, is greyish brown in colour and smooth, though it becomes rougher when it's older. Its leaves are green and **heart-shaped**.

WHERE DOES IT GROW?
Lilac trees are rare in the wild, and you'll most commonly find them growing in towns and gardens. In the wild, they tend to grow on rocky hills, in hedgerows and along woodland edges.

SCIENTIFIC NAME
Syringa vulgaris

NICKNAMES
Lilac tree or shrub, pipe privet, pipe tree

HOW LONG DOES IT LIVE FOR?
More than 100 years!

PARTS YOU CAN EAT
Flowers

THE FORAGER'S DICTIONARY
HEART-SHAPED
When leaves are described as heart-shaped, this means they are shaped like the symbol that represents a love heart.

BEST TIME TO PICK IT The flowers are ready to pick in spring.

WHAT CAN YOU DO WITH IT?

Nibble on the fresh flowers

Lilac flowers make a fun snack to nibble on when you're out and about, and they have a unique floral, cranberry flavour. They're also good for you because they are rich in antioxidants.

Lilac lemonade

You can make a really delicious drink by mixing lilac flowers with fruits such as raspberries. This drink is also known as lilac lemonade.

Lilac allsorts

With lilac flowers, you could make jams, syrups, ice cream, battered fritters, crystallized sweets, cocktails, wine, lemonade, cakes, infused honeys, lilac sugar and more!

I DIDN'T KNOW THAT!

THE WOOD IS MUSICAL!

No, it doesn't sing. Instead, lilac wood is occasionally used to make musical instruments such as flutes, ukuleles and maracas.

SMELLING SWEET

Lilac flowers release a beautiful natural scent. This smells so good that it's a popular ingredient in perfumes, soaps and oils.

GENTLY DOES IT

Some flowers, such as gorse, can quite happily be heated, boiled and blasted without losing their colour. Others, such as lilac flowers, are far more fragile and will quickly lose their colour if you treat them roughly.

FORAGER'S CHALLENGE

1. Find and identify a lilac tree.

2. Kindly ask a friend or neighbour with a lilac tree if you may pick some flowers. In return, gift them some lilac lemonade.

BEAUTIFUL HEALERS

As well as being enjoyed for their beautiful colours and sweet floral smells, lilac flowers have been used for medicine, too. Herbalists thought that a drink made with the flowers could help fight off and keep away a serious disease known as malaria, which is passed to people by mosquitoes.

The flowers were also used to help heal rashes on the skin and to make people feel and smell more beautiful. Often in history, when a flower looked and smelled nice, people would rub themselves with it to try to make themselves equally lovely!

Later, scientists decided to use lilacs for something quite interesting and unexpected. Because the flowers are rich in antioxidants, they gave an extract of the lilac flowers to mice with spinal-cord injuries (damaged backs). The study found that the flowers reduced the inflammation and injuries in the mice's bodies, helping them to heal better!

THE STORY OF THE LILAC TREE, SYRINGA AND PAN

There was once a mischievous Greek god called Pan, who was said to have the legs and horns of a goat and the body of a human. One day, while walking in the woods, he fell head over heels in love with a beautiful nymph (a magical woodland being) named Syringa. Instead of introducing himself like a gentlemen, Pan rushed at Syringa, scaring her and making her run away. In fact, she was so scared that once she was out of his sight, she transformed herself into a beautiful lilac tree.

Pan searched all over the woods trying to find Syringa, but he had no success and eventually gave up. Tired from all his hunting, he sat down next to a beautiful new tree he had never seen before. You guessed it – it was the lilac tree! Without knowing that the tree was actually Syringa, he cut a few of the hollow branches and used the wood to make his very first 'pan pipe', which he carried with him from then on.

So, it's all thanks to this Greek myth that part of the Latin name for the lilac is *Syringa*, named after the beautiful nymph who turned herself into the first ever lilac tree in order to escape Pan.

There are a few different versions of this myth. We've chosen just one of the stories we've found, and while it may not be the original one, we still think it's a cracking tale!

⚠️

Make sure you pay very close attention
to the information in the following pages.
It's really important to understand
poisonous plants and the dangers they pose.

Poisonous plants play an important role in the balance of our
natural world. They are also rich in some epic history and
folklore. But as foragers, it's our job to make sure we don't
accidentally eat them. This means we need to learn about
poisonous plants so we can avoid their dangers.

It can also be fun! When you come across these
plants in real life, you can share your
awesome knowledge with friends
and family . . .

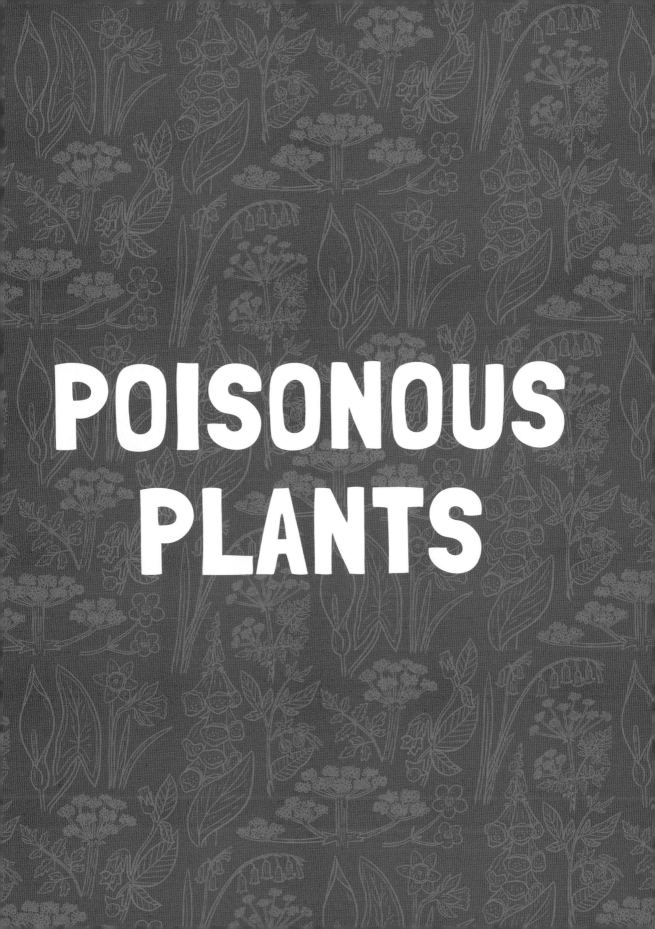

POISONOUS PLANTS

HINTS AND TIPS FOR POISONOUS PLANTS

Being scared of eating poisonous plants can sometimes put people off foraging, and this is only natural! At first glance, learning to forage may seem a bit tricky and confusing. Don't worry – it won't take you long to get your head around everything, and soon you'll find it pretty easy to successfully identify plants and trees, and feel confident enough to eat them.

We've talked about safety in the Ten Foraging Commandments section of the book (see pages 15-20), but here's a quick recap of the main rules to follow:

1. If in doubt, don't eat it!

2. Be wary of lookalikes

Some plants and trees look quite similar, so when you find a plant that you think may be edible, double-check before eating it.

3. Beginners should avoid plants in the carrot family (Apiaceae)

You might be surprised to learn that many relatives of the bright orange vegetable we call the carrot are seriously poisonous. These include one of the most poisonous plants in the world: hemlock water dropwort. It makes total sense, then, that most foragers choose not to forage for any plants in this family! Luckily, this is easy to do: just avoid plants that have feathery, fern-like leaves and white flower umbels. (We tell you more about umbels on page 112). You can rest assured that no edible plants in this book are in the carrot family. Phew!

4. Health and safety

Don't touch electric or barbed-wire fences! Stick to paths as much as possible and be respectful of livestock in fields. Make sure someone has a charged mobile phone and that you've planned your route. A little first-aid kit for bumps, stings and scrapes is handy, and check you've got any medication you may need while out (for instance, an adrenaline pen or insulin injector). Remember, you might be out for longer than you planned.

5. Know what to do in an emergency

Although it's unlikely that you'll eat something poisonous, it's best to know what to do in an emergency, just in case. First, stay calm and ring 999 or head to the emergency department of the nearest hospital. It's important to either bring a piece of the plant or tree that's been eaten with you or to take photos of it so that the doctors know what they are dealing with. **It's worth keeping photos of the plants you consume anyway, just in case you have an allergic reaction to something later on.**

HEMLOCK

WHAT DOES IT LOOK LIKE? Hemlock can grow up to around 3 m tall! That's bigger than any wrestler you might see on TV. Its stem is smooth and usually covered in purple spots and splashes. Its leaves are finely divided and grow to a large size, making an overall triangle shape. Its flowers are small, white and grow in **umbels** (see page 112).

WHERE DOES IT GROW? Hemlock can be found growing in woodlands, across grasslands and along field edges, pathways and roadsides.

SCIENTIFIC NAME *Conium maculatum*

NICKNAMES Wild hemlock, poison parsley, poison hemlock

THIS MUST NOT BE EATEN BECAUSE . . . All parts of this plant are extremely poisonous. Just eating a tiny bit can be fatal. It is especially dangerous because poisoning can occur just by handling the plant for a while. Symptoms of poisoning can include nausea, vomiting, tummy pain, dizziness and weakness. Worse, it affects our muscles, causing paralysis that means you can't breathe and may go into a coma or die.

HOW TO AVOID IT Just like giant hogweed (see page 195), hemlock has the same unique stem covered in purple spots and splashes, meaning it's easy to spot. Similar to hemlock water dropwort (see page 192), the plant also has leaves that look a bit like parsley, and the white flower umbels are typical of the dreaded carrot family.

A HISTORY OF POISON

In ancient Greece, hemlock was used to poison prisoners who had been sentenced to death. A very well-known and wise man named Socrates was the most famous victim of hemlock poisoning. He was accused of leading the young men of Athens astray and was sentenced to death in 399 BCE. Poison hemlock was the method chosen. A drink was made from the plant, which Socrates consumed. He died soon after.

LORDS-AND-LADIES

WHAT DOES IT LOOK LIKE? The plant begins to pop up in late winter and quickly grows large arrow-shaped leaves with deep lobes at the bottom where the leaf joins the stem. These leaves are shiny green and can have dark purple spots on them. If you look closely at a leaf, you can see that the veins stop before they reach the edge, creating a rim round the outside of the leaf without veins. This is unique to these plants. When these leaves die back after flowering, an upright stalk is revealed. Clusters of berries grow from this stalk and turn bright red or orange.

WHERE DOES IT GROW? Lords-and-ladies loves shade, and you'll find it covering the floors of woodlands, under hedgerows and scattered around towns and gardens.

SCIENTIFIC NAME *Arum maculatum*

NICKNAMES Cuckoo pint, Adam and Eve, devils and angels

THIS MUST NOT BE EATEN BECAUSE . . . This plant is full of tiny needle-shaped crystals which, as soon as they're chewed or rubbed into the skin, cause a painful burning, itchy feeling. This can result in swelling and might even cause breathing difficulties. The most common way people are affected by the plant is by accidentally using the leaves as toilet roll!

HOW TO AVOID IT Lords-and-ladies grows in lots of places, so it's very important you get to know the plant. Its leaves can be mistaken for wild garlic, dock or burdock, so make sure you compare and learn the difference between the four plants. Remember the tip about the unique unveined rim round the edge of the leaf – this will be really helpful in identifying what is a lords-and-ladies leaf, and what isn't.

HEMLOCK WATER DROPWORT

WHAT DOES IT LOOK LIKE? Hemlock water dropwort looks similar to many other members of the carrot family, such as parsley and wild celery. The plant is hairless and can grow to around 1.5 m tall. Its leaves are bright green, shiny and triangular in shape. Its flowers are white and grow in umbels. After these flowers have died back, seed heads (the part of a plant that contains the seeds) form, which are a dark brown in colour. The hemlock's stem is hollow and grooved, with the grooves running vertically up the stem.

WHERE DOES IT GROW? As the 'water' bit of its name suggests, this plant is most often found growing alongside rivers, streams and lakes or in ditches and damp, marshy ground.

SCIENTIFIC NAME *Oenanthe crocata*

NICKNAMES Water hemlock, dead man's fingers, dead tongue

THIS MUST NOT BE EATEN BECAUSE . . . This plant is considered to be one of the deadliest in the world. Consuming it can cause horrible symptoms, such as nausea, vomiting, seizures and hallucinations. Worst of all, it can make your muscles constrict, or tighten up, which means you can't breathe and could die by suffocation.

HOW TO AVOID IT If you want to completely dodge any chances of having an unwanted encounter with this plant, or any plants in its deadly carrot family, avoid foraging for plants with white umbel flowers.

WOODY NIGHTSHADE

WHAT DOES IT LOOK LIKE? This plant has pretty, bright purple, star-shaped flowers from late spring until mid-autumn. These have five petals and yellow stamens that stick out from the petals. After flowering, it has round berries that begin life a bright green colour but later turn bright red. These berries hang in clusters. Its leaves are small, green and arrowhead-shaped.

WHERE DOES IT GROW? Woody nightshade is a crawling plant, meaning you'll most likely find it tangled within other plants. It's most commonly found along hedges, pathways and in woodlands.

SCIENTIFIC NAME *Solanum dulcamara*

NICKNAMES Bittersweet, scarlet berry, trailing nightshade, violet bloom

THIS MUST NOT BE EATEN BECAUSE . . . Woody nightshade is in the same family as the famous deadly nightshade (see page 198) but it's less poisonous. However, it still shouldn't be messed around with. If it's accidentally consumed, the symptoms are an itchy throat, dizziness, dilated (big) pupils and difficulty speaking and breathing. It can even potentially lead to death!

HOW TO AVOID IT Woody nightshade is a good example of why we should always pay attention when foraging. The berries look like little sweet tomatoes and can be very appealing. The plant can also grow wrapped within other bushes such as blackberries, so you might accidentally pick some of the berries along with your blackberries. Pay attention while picking and don't shovel blackberries or raspberries into your mouth without looking at them first!

DAFFODIL

WHAT DOES IT LOOK LIKE? This distinctive spring flower grows to about 50 cm tall. Its leaves are narrow and a green-grey colour. Its flower head has bright yellow or white petals and is shaped like a trumpet.

WHERE DOES IT GROW? Daffodils appear in spring in woodlands, towns and gardens.

SCIENTIFIC NAME *Narcissus* (we've only included the genus here, as there are many different species of daffodil)

NICKNAMES Lent lily

THIS MUST NOT BE EATEN BECAUSE . . . If you accidentally eat any part of a daffodil, it will cause a painful upset stomach and, in rare cases, death.

HOW TO AVOID IT Daffodil poisoning is rare. When it does happen, it's usually because the bulb was mistaken for an onion. To avoid this mistake, don't grow daffodils next to vegetable patches!

THE LEGEND OF NARCISSUS

The daffodil's scientific name comes from an ancient Greek legend about a man called Narcissus. One day, Narcissus was looking at his own reflection in a pool of water and liked what he saw so much that he fell in love with himself! He became so obsessed with his own reflection that he never left, and stared at it constantly, forgetting to eat or sleep. He eventually became so tired and weak that he fell in the pool and drowned. It was said that the first ever daffodil grew at the spot where Narcissus drowned, and that the reason why the flowers lean forwards is because they are mimicking Narcissus as he leaned over the pool.

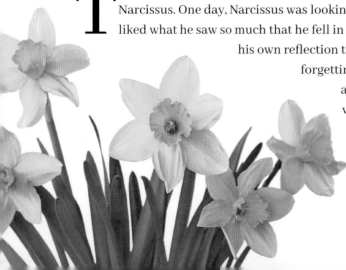

GIANT HOGWEED

WHAT DOES IT LOOK LIKE?

Giant hogweed lives up to its name! It grows to a huge size – sometimes over 5 m high. Its large, shiny green leaves are divided into smaller leaflets with serrated lobes. Its flowers are small and white, and they grow in umbels. The stems are tall, green, thick and covered in purply-red blotches with stiff white bristly hairs. These stems are particularly hairy around the base of each leaf stalk and are hollow inside.

WHERE DOES IT GROW?
Giant hogweed likes to grow in damp places, such as along riverbanks, streams and canals and on boggy wastelands.

SCIENTIFIC NAME
Heracleum mantegazzianum

NICKNAMES
Cartwheel flower, giant cow parsley, giant cow parsnip, hogsbane

THIS MUST NOT BE EATEN BECAUSE . . .
Giant hogweed is poisonous to eat, but what's most dangerous is its sap. When this comes into contact with our skin it causes severe burns and blisters. Even once the burn has healed, a patch of damaged skin will be left behind that is more likely to be damaged by the sun's UV rays.

HOW TO AVOID IT
It's pretty easy to identify giant hogweed when it's fully grown because of its unique stem, which is covered in purply-red blotches. But when the plant is younger, it just looks like simple leaves growing low to the ground. So, again, always make sure you are confident about identifying young green leaves before picking any.

POISONOUS PEA SHOOTERS

The plant became well known in the 1970s because children started to come home with burns and blisters. People realized that the plant had become popular with children because of its strong, hollow stems, which the children were cutting to use as telescopes and pea shooters!

FOXGLOVE

WHAT DOES IT LOOK LIKE? Foxgloves are tall plants with beautiful flowers. Once you learn what they look like, you'll start to notice them everywhere during the summer. The plant grows up to around 2.5 m tall and often has bright pink flowers, though they can also be purple, lavender, yellow or white. When you look closely inside the flowers, you'll see they have little spotty markings which help guide insects to the heart of the flower to collect nectar and pollen. Its leaves are soft, green and lanceolate-shaped (narrowing to a point at each end).

WHERE DOES IT GROW? Foxgloves are common. You'll often find them growing in open grasslands, open woodlands, wastelands and in gardens.

SCIENTIFIC NAME *Digitalis purpurea*

NICKNAMES There are loads, including common foxglove, witches' gloves, bloody bells, dead men's bells, cow flop, lion's mouth . . .

THIS MUST NOT BE EATEN BECAUSE . . . Accidentally eating foxgloves can cause lots of problems. Symptoms include sickness, headache, skin irritation, vomiting, dizziness, abdominal pain and diarrhoea. In severe cases, it can cause vision to turn green and lead to heart failure.

HOW TO AVOID IT When the foxglove is fully grown in summer it's pretty easy to avoid as it's fairly obvious what it is. The only plant it looks a bit similar to is rosebay willowherb (see page 84), though it's simple enough to tell the difference between the two because foxglove flowers are bell-shaped, whereas rosebay willowherb flowers look like flat, open stars. When the foxglove is a young plant, though, it grows low to the ground and looks like a bundle of leaves. Always make sure you are confident about identifying plain young green leaves before eating any.

HEART-STOPPING MEDICINE

One of the foxglove's common names is dead men's bells, which comes from the fact that if we consume too much of the plant our hearts stop. In the past, herbalists used foxgloves to treat heart conditions. These herbal remedies were very dangerous and many people died from taking them.

FOX . . . GLOVES?

The most common name for these plants comes from a time long ago, when people believed that fairies made foxglove flowers for the foxes to wear on their paws. This was said to give them the ability to sneak around in silence so they couldn't be heard when they were stealing chickens. It was also said that the little spots you see within the foxglove flowers were the handprints of the fairies themselves.

DEADLY NIGHTSHADE

WHAT DOES IT LOOK LIKE? Luckily for us, deadly nightshade is pretty easy to identify with its purple, downward-hanging bell-shaped flowers. Its leaves are green and oval-shaped with smooth edges and a pointed tip. The berries are round and a deep shade of black that shines like the pupils of our eyes.

WHERE DOES IT GROW? It's quite rare to find the deadly nightshade plant growing in the wild in the UK. You'll most likely see it along pathways, in undisturbed areas and through hedgerows.

SCIENTIFIC NAME *Atropa belladonna*

NICKNAMES Belladonna

THIS MUST NOT BE EATEN BECAUSE . . . Deadly nightshade is one of the most poisonous plants known to humankind! All parts of this plant are deadly poisonous. If someone was to accidentally consume deadly nightshade, their pupils would dilate (become larger), their speech would become slurred, they'd start to feel confused and begin hallucinating and then fall into a coma and die. You must **not** touch it.

HOW TO AVOID IT Deadly nightshade poisoning is rare because the plant itself is quite uncommon. To avoid potentially eating it, always make sure you compare any flower, leaves or berries you haven't eaten before with photos of deadly nightshade to make sure you can tell the difference between them. As ever, if you're not 100 per cent sure, don't eat it!

BLIND BEAUTY

Deadly nightshade is so powerfully poisonous that you'd think everyone throughout history did their best to avoid it, right? Wrong! Over in Italy, the plant was once seen as a beauty product. People would put some of the plant in water to infuse, then ladies would drop this water into their eyes! This made their pupils get bigger, which they thought looked beautiful. This beauty treatment would, not surprisingly, damage their eyes and using it over a long period would cause blindness.

THE POWER TO FLY

Hubble, bubble, this plant is definitely trouble. You know why? Because it's said to be the main ingredient witches would use to make their broomsticks fly! Witches would supposedly make an ointment from a mixture of deadly nightshade, opium, bat's blood and the fat of young children, and then smear it on their broomsticks. We don't recommend you try this at home . . .

BUTTERCUP

WHAT DOES IT LOOK LIKE? Buttercups come in many different shapes and sizes, though they all look very similar. The important thing to know is that none of them are edible! Buttercups usually flower in the spring but can also be found throughout the summer. Their leaves tend to be hairy and divided into three to five lobes. Often, the leaves grow in a rosette (in a circle at the base of the stem). The flowers are bright yellow, almost golden, in colour, with a cluster of bright yellow stamens. The petals of buttercups are often so smooth and shiny that anything close to them ends up looking yellow!

WHERE DOES IT GROW? Like daisies, you'll find buttercups growing pretty much everywhere, from gardens and parks to fields and meadows.

SCIENTIFIC NAME *Ranunculus acris*

NICKNAMES Meadow buttercup, tall buttercup

THIS MUST NOT BE EATEN BECAUSE . . . If you eat buttercups, they may cause painful mouth blisters and upset your stomach. They don't taste of butter!

HOW TO AVOID IT It's easy to not eat buttercups because they look so unique. Just remember not to eat those shiny golden flowers!

DO YOU LIKE BUTTER?

The name buttercup comes from a time when people believed that if cows ate buttercups, it turned their butter yellow. There's also an old game you can play with buttercups. Hold the flower under your or a friend's chin, and see if the chin glows yellow. If it does, this is said to mean that you love butter! Whereas if your chin refuses to shine, this means you hate it.

THE STORY OF THE MISER

There is an old story of how the buttercup came into this world. There was once a greedy man who hoarded gold but hated to spend any of it on things such as new clothes or getting his hair cut. Every room of his house was full to the brim with gold – even his bed was stuffed with it!

One day, the old man was walking home across a meadow with his latest bag of gold. This caught the attention of some fairies who were building their house. The fairies needed a roof for their new home and thought that a gold coin would be strong and waterproof. So, they decided to politely ask the old man for just one coin. In response, the old man, angry at the request, shouted 'NO!' and swung his bag of gold at the fairies to scare them away.

The fairies decided to teach the old man a lesson and cast a spell on him: 'From this day on, whatever bag you own will have a hole in it, making you drop coins wherever you go. These coins will turn into golden flowers so you shall never find them again'. From that day on, every coin that fell from the old man's bag turned into a shiny golden buttercup, covering the land wherever he roamed.

BLUEBELL

WHAT DOES IT LOOK LIKE? Bluebells have flowers that are a bluish-purple colour with six petals and upturned tips. These flowers droop to one side of their single stem, making them look a bit like dangling bells. If you peer closely into the flowers, you'll see they contain creamy-coloured pollen. The leaves are long, narrow and smooth with pointed tips. They smell wonderful and are pretty hard to miss. If you're lucky, you might find a rare white albino bluebell, and they are also sometimes pink.

WHERE DOES IT GROW? Bluebells tend to grow in woodlands and forests but are also a popular plant in gardens.

SCIENTIFIC NAME *Hyacinthoides non-scripta*

NICKNAMES Cuckoo's boots, witches' thimbles, lady's nightcap, fairy flower

THIS MUST NOT BE EATEN BECAUSE . . . All parts of a bluebell are poisonous. If it is eaten, it can cause stomach upset and pain and could even be fatal.

HOW TO AVOID IT Bluebell flowers are bright blue, so it's pretty easy to spot them when they're in flower. However, before bluebells flower, they look similar to edible plants such as wild garlic. To avoid accidentally eating them, only forage for plain green leaves if you are 100 per cent confident you can correctly identify them.

BLUEBELL FOLKLORE

Folklore says that bluebell woods are the enchanted homes of fairies. The story goes that at dawn each day, the bluebells ring like little bells to call the fairies back home. If a person is unlucky enough to hear this ringing, then they shall die soon after. It is also said that if you are spotted picking bluebells, then fairies will come and lead you away, never to be seen again!

BLUEBELL PROTECTION

As well as the fact that they're poisonous (and the fairies might get you!), another reason not to dig up bluebells is that it's against the law in the UK. In fact, if someone is caught selling wild bluebell bulbs then they can be fined £5,000!

CONNECTING WITH NATURE

We often hear that it's important to 'reconnect' with nature. But what does this actually mean, and how can we do it?

It's simple, really – just get outside and try things! Connecting with nature can be as easy as going for a walk in the woods, a park or along a river. Or it could be a more long-term project such as growing your own food. It's all about finding what's right for you.

Whatever you choose to do is likely to be beneficial. When we go out into the natural world, it not only helps our own health and well-being, but it's also good for nature. We get to take a break from our busy lives, screens, traffic, noise and stress, and feel better in our minds and bodies. Along the way, we increase our understanding and love of the natural world. It's a win–win situation.

In this chapter, we want to share what we've learned on our own journey. We explore ways to connect with nature through forest bathing, show how to create mindful memories, and give loads of ideas for fun things to do while you are out and about. Enjoy!

Follow your heart, it will lead you somewhere.

THE ART OF FOREST BATHING

What exactly is forest bathing? It sounds wild, right? Taking a bath or shower in the forest? In fact, forest bathing is a health and mindfulness practice that first started in Japan in the 1980s. There, it is called *shinrin-yoku*, which means 'taking in the forest atmosphere' or 'forest bathing'.

Forest bathing is all about spending time being at one with woodlands or forests, paying full attention to the natural world around us. Quite often, when we go on walks, we charge through the woods at top speed, thinking about everything apart from our surroundings. 'Will I get that piece of work done on time?', 'Where did I put that sock?' or 'I wonder what we're going to do at the weekend?' We tend to walk the same route over and over again, paying less and less attention because it's so familiar. Of course this is great exercise, and there's nothing wrong with it, but how often do we pause and really take in the natural world?

And that's what forest bathing is: purposefully giving yourself the gift of time to disconnect from daily life and reconnect with nature – to listen to the birds, notice the changing seasons and breathe in deeply. And . . . relax.

There is no WiFi in the forest, but you'll be sure to find a better connection.

HOW TO FOREST BATHE

The first thing you need to do to forest bathe is get out into some woods or a forest. If you live in a town or city, then a group of trees in a park is better than nothing, though a larger wood or forest is ideal. Mindfully notice what's going on around you using your senses of sight, hearing, taste, smell and touch. Try to stay in the present moment, rather than thinking about other stuff. Below are some tips on how to do it:

- **Head to a wood, forest or a group of trees**

- **Turn off your devices**

- **Walk or move slowly**

- **Look closely at the environment around you**

- **Take deep breaths**

- **Engage all your senses**

- **Take off your shoes (if the ground isn't muddy or spiky!)**

- **Stop, stand or sit**

- **Keep thinking about the present moment (this is called mindfulness)**

- **Head off the main path and explore little side paths**

- **See what's over the horizon**

- **Have a picnic**

- **Watch the birds**

- **Touch the trees**

- **Play the Five Senses Game (see page 211)**

- **Look up at the sky and notice the clouds**

- **Forage for some food**

- **Bring a flask of tea and enjoy a cup**

CREATING MINDFUL MEMORIES

Lots of grown-ups look back on their childhood memories as special things that can never be experienced again. This sense of longing for the past is called *hiraeth* in Welsh and can make people feel a little bit sad.

But the main reason why memories of childhood experiences are so strong is not because they happened during childhood, but because children are much better at living in the present and paying attention to what's going on around them. Adults are far too easily distracted by thinking about boring things, yacking on their phones, or listening to podcasts or music instead of nature.

Children are also much better at exploring the world with all their senses. They watch the colours of the sky transform as the sun sets, part overgrown shrubs to see what's hiding underneath and smell the scents of the crushed foliage underfoot. All this while listening to the birds singing as they munch on wild blackberries, thinking only about what lies over the horizon.

So, your challenge is to get the adults in your life to be more like you! Ask them to stop adulting and to play the Five Senses Game as you go on walks together. They'll thank you for it, and together you'll create new happy memories.

THE FIVE SENSES GAME

This game comes from the world of mindfulness. By playing it, we deliberately use all our senses one by one. This helps to bring us into the present moment and to experience the natural world in a deeper, more powerful way. The great thing about this game is that it's super simple to play, either on your own or with friends and family, whenever you're out in nature. Not everybody has five senses (if you are blind or Deaf, for example), so lean into the senses you do have and enjoy.

All you have to do is ask these simple questions:

1. What can you see?
Stand still and name a few things that catch your eye. For instance, flower blossoms are beautiful, so have a closer look! What do they really look like? How many petals do they have? Are there any bugs in the flowers? If you're lucky, you may come across a sleeping bee. *Shhh!*

2. What can you hear?
Stop and listen. Close your eyes and tune into your ears. Are the trees rustling in the wind? Can you hear the birds singing? How far away do they sound?

3. What can you feel?
Pause to explore what nature feels like to the touch. Notice how the moss is soft like a blanket or how the sap oozing from a tree is super sticky.

4. What can you smell?
Breathe in the scents of nature. Sniff the flowers, crush some leaves to release their essential oils and smell the scents of juicy wild fruits. Or take deep lungfuls of that lovely fresh air you find among trees.

5. What can you taste?
Use your knowledge to forage and taste the edible species of plants and trees, from juicy fruits to crunchy flowers and leaves. **Ask an adult** to take along a flask of hot water, add some plants and make a fresh herbal tea. Then sit with the plants you made it from as you drink it.

NATURE IS GOOD FOR US

According to new research by the Royal Society for the Protection of Birds, only one in five children in the UK has a regular connection with nature and spends time playing outdoors.

Another study, this time conducted by the National Trust, found that even the language of nature is being gradually lost. And yet now more than ever, we need to have the ability to disconnect from the modern world. This is difficult with so many shiny gadgets around that have been designed to grab and keep our attention. These screens make our brains release the feel-good chemicals that give us the same feeling of gratification we get when opening a Christmas present.

The goal isn't to be anti-technology. Technology can be a beautiful thing when it's used in the right way. But this endless quest to keep attention on screens isn't good for our well-being. And what has been proven to be good for our well-being? Nature! There's a reason why the sound of rain falling and birds singing is soothing – it's meant to be a part of our life experience. We are animals, after all.

We've learned during our journey to pick our battles and find a balance that's right for us. Building a connection to nature doesn't have to be a chore that involves grimly heading outdoors in all weathers, but it does take effort. The key is to find things you enjoy: a walk through the woods that ends at a cafe that sells chips and ice cream or a promise of a picnic really can make all the difference.

Try not to feel disheartened if it's just the thought of the ice cream keeping you going! You'll often find that once you arrive in the great outdoors any worries you have about being outdoors or away from a screen will melt away, just like the ice cream you're thinking about! The more you get out in nature, the more you'll naturally feel wild and free.

THINGS TO DO IN NATURE

We all love a walk, but there are so many other activities to enjoy outside. We've written a list of activities we like doing together in the fresh air, but can you think of any others? Lots of the activities below require an adult's supervision, so be sure to ask for help before getting started.

- Fly a kite
- Walk barefoot
- Climb trees
- Go camping
- Have a picnic
- Build a fort
- Feed wild animals
- Climb a big hill
- Roll down a big hill
- Book a stay in interesting accommodation (there are some great tree houses out there)
- Ride a bike
- Go canoeing or kayaking
- Get to know a tree or animal well and visit it often
- Put your feet in some water
- Skim stones across a river
- Drop sticks into a river and watch them race along
- Put on wellies and walk through mud
- Look for fish
- Learn to identify birds and their songs

- Make things from mud and sticks
- Make a crown with flowers
- Create wild art
- Find shapes in the clouds
- Watch the sunrise or sunset
- Go for a walk at night
- Go stargazing
- Look for fossils and bones
- Organize a scavenger hunt
- Look for bugs
- Make homes for wildlife
- Make wildlife feeders
- Plant a tree
- Go swimming in the sea
- Learn to use a paper map
- Cook over a fire
- Go to countryside markets
- Balance on a slackline between trees
- Join a forest school
- Grow some vegetables

NATURE IS OUR HOME

As American environmentalist and poet Gary Snyder once said: 'Nature isn't a place to visit. It is home'. It doesn't matter whether you're a bushcraft lover who gets their fresh air while building a camp, or a punk rocker with flowers in their hair who loves to sing with the birds, we all come from the same place, and to spend time in nature is to spend time in our true home. We must take care of it, respect it and love it just as we do each other.

ACKNOWLEDGEMENTS

THANK YOU FOR READING!

From the bottom of our hearts, we thank you for reading our book! We hope it brings you lots of fresh air and sunshine and many happy memories. If you're old enough to be on social media, make sure to check us out online at Home Is Where Our Heart Is on YouTube, Facebook and Instagram so you can watch our videos and stay connected! We'd also love to thank the amazing illustrators, proofreaders and team at Puffin who have made this book possible: Elly Jahnz, Sophie Stericker, Susanne Masters, Corinne Lucas, Philippa Neville, Tom Rawlinson, Sarah Connelly, Katy Finch, Kimberley Davis, Claire Davis and Lucy Doncaster.

This space is reserved for you to note down your Forager's Challenge scores as you complete the tasks. Remember: each time you complete a quest, you get one Knowledge Point. Simple!

House Mouse
Your foraging skills tend to lead you to the fridge.

0–10 POINTS

Field Mouse
Your foraging skills are good enough to provide you with an outside snack.

11–20 POINTS

Squirrel
Your foraging knowledge is fair; you can tumble through the countryside collecting wild food as you go.

21–30 POINTS

Hedgehog
You've got a skilful foraging eye.

31–40 POINTS

Badger
Your foraging knowledge is now so advanced that you can officially forage enough food to keep you full for ages!

41–50 POINTS

Fox
A seasoned forager, there's not much you don't know about the wild.

51–60 POINTS

Gold Crest
You are now a true foraging master.

61+ POINTS

CONVERSION CHARTS

Use this for converting any liquids from cups to millilitres.

CUP	MILLILITRES
1	250
1/2	125
1/3	83
1/4	62.5

Use this for converting any solids (such as nuts or loose leaves) from cups to millilitres.

CUP	MILLILITRES
1	225
1/2	118
1/3	79
1/4	59

Use these tables for converting key recipe ingredients (butter, flour and sugar) from cups to grams.

Butter

CUP	GRAMS
1	225
1/2	112
1/4	55

Flour

CUP	GRAMS
1	250
1/2	64
1/4	32

Sugar

CUP	GRAMS
1	200
1/2	100
1/4	50

GLOSSARY

Ailments An illness – normally quite a small one!

Biodiversity All the different living things you'll find in a certain area.

Dye A natural or human-made substance used to add a colour to, or change the colour of, something.

Floral Relating to flowers.

Flowering Producing or bearing flowers.

Folklore and folktales The traditional beliefs, customs and stories of a community, passed through the generations by word of mouth.

Harvest The process of gathering crops.

Hedgerows A line of bushes or shrubs planted to make a natural barrier, like a fence. These hedgerows provide food for wildlife (and foragers!).

Inflammation A physical condition in which part of the body becomes reddened, swollen, hot and often painful, especially in reaction to an injury or infection.

Mythology A collection of myths (stories), in particular those dealing with the gods and goddesses of a particular people (the Greek Myths, for instance).

Native Someone or something that is born, or comes from, a particular area.

Nutritious Contains substances our bodies need to stay healthy.

Pollination The act of transferring pollen grains from the male part of the flower to the female part.

Scrubland An area of land covered with low trees and bushes.

Stem The main body or stalk of a plant or shrub.

Sustainability Maintaining conditions under which humans and nature can co-exist.

YOUR FORAGING NOTES